The Mirror of Wond
and o

The Mirror of Wonders and other tales

SYED RAFIQ HUSSAIN

Translated by
Saleem Kidwai

YODAPRESS

YODA PRESS
268 A/C, Vasant Kunj
New Delhi 110 070
www.yodapress.com

ISBN 978-93-80403-09-0

Editor in-charge: Prakriti Mukerjee
Typeset in Dante MT 10.5/14
By Jojy Philip, New Delhi 110 015
Printed at Chaman Offset Printers, New Delhi 110 002
Published by Arpita Das for YODA PRESS

For Kabir and Emaad

Contents

Introduction

The writings of Syed Rafiq Hussain were first published in the literary journal *Saqi*.[1] The eight stories translated here were his only writings that were subsequently published as a volume, *Aina e Hairat*.[2] However, his writings had almost disappeared from circulation till 2002 when most of them were published again.[3] These include an incomplete work which was probably meant to be a novel, related editorial material and writings about him that had been published in a special edition of the literary journal *Naya Daur* (Karachi, Vols 45–46, June 1968). Also included in this collection are two articles by Nayyar Masood published in *Saughat* (Bangalore, Vol. 5, September 1993). Most of the pieces about Hussain are recollections of relatives, friends and acquaintances. The present biographical note is based entirely on the materials published in *Naya Daur*.

Here is an autobiographical sketch that Hussain wrote from the same volume:

[1] *Saqi* was started by Shahid Ahmad Dehlavi (b. 1906) from Delhi in January 1930 and continued to be published till 1947 when the editor migrated to Pakistan. The journal resumed publication from Karachi in September 1948 and continued until his death in 1967.

[2] Published by Saqi Book Depot, Delhi, 1944. This collection was published twice again but under different names. *Sher Kya Sochta Hoga* (Kitabghar Publications, Rampur, UP n.d.) and *Gori ho Gori* (Urdu Academy Sindh, Karachi, 1952).

[3] *Aina e Hairat aur Doosri Tehreeren* (City Press Book Shop, Karachi, 2002).

About Myself[4]

I was born in Lucknow in 1895. My mother died when I was seven and my childhood was very disturbed. Sometimes I lived with my sister, sometimes with an aunt and at other times with sundry relatives. When my father remarried, life became settled again. By then, my education had been completely disrupted and this was never remedied. I was never considered a good student in school.

In 1915—when we all were with my father who was posted in Etawah and while I was studying in the 9th class, I ran away to Bombay without informing anyone at home. For six months I worked in a washing factory. I used to work all day and study at night. I, then, sat for the entrance exam of an Engineering institute. I was selected and informed my family who started to send me money and I began to study in earnest. In 1920 I finished my engineering degree. From then till now, I have been periodically employed. This is my eighteenth job. In none of the jobs were my employers unhappy with my work, nor did they willingly let me go. It is a weakness in my nature that I cannot work at a job for long. Currently, I have given the government three successive notices that I want to quit my job and that they should arrange for a replacement but they haven't found the right man and my officers are unwilling to let me go.

My job consigned me to the jungles of the Terai *for over a dozen years. I have also roamed the Indian Ocean as an engineer on a ship and during these wanderings even performed my Hajj. But by looking at me, no one would ever guess that I am a Haji. I have been wearing short pants and a white short-sleeved shirt from the time I was ten, till today.*

I cannot write Urdu at all. I am very weak at spelling. Except for my daughter, no one, not even I myself, can read my handwriting. When I am in the mood and when my imaginary plots are dying to reach paper

[4] *Aina e Hairat aur Doosri Tehreeren*, pp. 323–25. This was originally published in *Mera Behtareen Afsana*, ed., Bashir Hindi (Lahore n.d.).

through my pen, I write, and sometimes spelling even the simplest of words takes me a couple of minutes. I must have read about four or five books in Urdu. I have never studied Persian but can speak it and even write short compositions in it. However, I cannot read a sentence of written Persian. I have read a lot in English. I must have read over two thousand novels and stories in English. My memory is very weak. Not only do I forget people's names but what is more troubling is remembering people's faces. If someone whom I have spent years with but have not seen for six months suddenly appears before me, I go aflutter. This is the reason why I am reluctant to meet people or socialize. I hate animals. I have never willingly allowed the presence of a pet animal in the house.

People must want to know when and why I started writing in Urdu. My daughter and younger sister are very interested in Urdu literature. A few years ago they praised highly a short story published in some magazine and enthusiastically began to read it to me. I left in the middle of the reading and this angered both of them. I said the difference between English and Urdu literature was like that between a spinning wheel and a cotton mill or a bullock-cart and a train. So why did I need to listen to that story when I only enjoyed reading literature in English? They labelled this a manifestation of my slave mentality and admonished me for my indifference to my mother tongue. They also challenged me—if I had such a poor opinion of the standards of Urdu literature, why did I not do something to improve them? Therefore, on their insistence, I started to write and soon my essays and stories began to be appreciated. I cannot claim that my pieces are artistically complete but since I have deeply observed a variety of literary elegances you will definitely see flashes of talent in my writings. I can write without knowing the language. Perhaps this is a grace consequent on being from Lucknow.

In English literature even if seventy-five per cent of writings concern love and romance, there is at least twenty-five per cent that deal with other issues. However in Urdu, the obsession with love and romance is two hundred per cent. It appears that almost everything else is excluded. I have, therefore, decided never to write about love and romance. I draw up a plot and check out all the details in my mind before I write. 'Kalua', based on a dog of that name, is my first story. Before I wrote it I walked all those streets and lanes of Lucknow where Kalua had wandered. The details of the railway crossing at Aish Bagh, where Kalua sniffs at the corpse of his mentor Bucha,[5] *are still etched in my mind.*

Among writers I like Tolstoy the most. I cannot imagine life without art.

This autobiographical sketch succeeds in what every storyteller aims to do—create an enigmatic character and arouse curiosity about his circumstances. Here was an Urdu writer who claimed not to know how to write Urdu 'at all', yet who created gems in a genre till then unknown to Urdu literature; an Urdu speaker who, without studying it, could speak and compose in Persian but not read it; a man who claimed to hate animals, yet observed them closely enough to write these empathetic 'animal-stories'; someone who proudly proclaimed his disdain for romance and claimed that he never wrote about love and romance, yet wrote two of the most striking love stories in Urdu: 'Shirin-Farhad' and 'The Voiceless' (*Bezubaan*). For one who had read 'four or five' books in Urdu, his confidence in pioneering a genre non-existent until then in Urdu literature displayed one of his important character-traits—arrogance.

He provided further autobiographical details in a piece of fiction he wrote. In the unfinished *Fasana-e Akbar*—a historical mystery narrated in the first person—he introduces himself as

[5] I translate this name as Missing-Ears.

a character who, one hot afternoon in Agra, steps back a few centuries into history when he descends into a Mughal step-well. This introduction is very much in the tradition of Perso-Urdu classical writings where authors introduced themselves and their work while invoking the name of God for blessings and assistance in telling the truth. It also leads into the narrative where facts and the strategies of a master storyteller are woven together to create an even more intriguing picture of himself.

Fasana-e Akbar[6]
(The Great Story of Akbar)

At the outset, I plead with you O God to help me write my life-story (aap beeti). *You are all powerful, so give fluency to the pen of one as ignorant as me; give my writing clarity so that I, with courage and candour, can truthfully describe without prejudice the events I know to be true. I ask for nothing more. Readers can make what they want of this and frankly I don't care what they think. The truth is that when I look back, I am confused myself. Only God knows what the truth is because my intellect has no answer. Perhaps, one of the readers can unravel this mystery. If this be so, let God be praised.*

I am under the overpowering illusion that this exercise will lead to the disclosure of some great universal secret. It is with this in mind that I have begun to write this story. My writings will have other benefits too. I will be able to clarify matters as far as possible for my relatives, friends and government officials. I have avoided this until now and this has resulted in increased misunderstandings for all of them have created their own suspicions of me. The government suspects me of being a rebel or a spy; relatives make allegations about my character and friends charge me with

[6] pp. 252–261.

being a fraud. I will no longer hide anything from anyone and will lay before all what has befallen me in the last year.

From the 3rd of June 1942 to the 1st July 1943, I was untraceable.[7] *Where I stayed, what I did, what befell me during this period I have written in this story. And since this is now going to be made public, I feel it is only appropriate that I introduce myself.*

I am from Lucknow and I was born in 1895. I was about seven when my mother passed away. My late father, Janab Khan Bahadur Syed Jafar Hussain Sahib had temporarily moved from the Government of the United Provinces to take over as State Engineer in the state of Gwalior. After my mother's death, we, that is, a sister a year older than me and another a year younger than me and I, became pawns in the game of grab played by our relatives. The result was that for four years I studied the Urdu alphabet and yet managed not to learn it. Phuphi Amma, my father's sister, may God bless her soul, managed to win one round and she grabbed all of us and took us with her to Lucknow. There, from dawn to seven in the morning and then from one in the afternoon until it was dark, I would sit on a bed-stead in front of a book-stand with the tattered Baghdadi Qaida[8] *on it (I cannot figure out why books of those days insisted on turning into shreds within a few days) and rock while I tried to memorize the alphabet. I would sit at one end of a long verandah and at the other end lay my paralyzed grandmother on her low cot like a bag of clothes, calling out, at intervals of five minutes, 'Ari Bafatun, won't you give me some areca nuts and tobacco?'*

Every half an hour or so Bafatun would come and stuff a fistful of tobacco and areca-nut-dust into my grandmother's mouth. We would be the only two in the verandah, both involved in our respective mutterings. My two sisters used to also sit here and learn to read the Quran in the

[7] This period when he 'went missing' he supposedly spent in the 'reign' of the Mughal emperor Akbar.

[8] A popular primer used to teach Urdu.

morning. One of them had already read the Quran and was now revising it. The other was about to complete it for the first time. They would read for an hour or so and then call out to my aunt, 'Phuphi Amma, shall we re-read it out to you?' From inside the room where she would be washing betel leaves my aunt would answer, 'Go ahead, read.' Since she had already memorized the Quran, she would correct them and add, 'Read it once again and you can go.' My sisters would be gone in a little while and Dadi Amma and I would be left in the verandah. She would softly repeat, 'Ari Bafita, will you give me something? Some areca nuts and tobacco?' I, while playing with the end of my draw-string, would keep repeating the alphabet. And neither Dadi nor I would dare stop our mutterings. If I stopped even for a moment my aunt would call out and ask if I had begun to play. And if my paralyzed Dadi Amma dozed off (which she sometimes did) and fell silent, Phuphi Amma would get startled and call out, 'Ari Bafatun, run and see what the matter is with Amma.' Bafatun would immediately come, shake the old lady and call back, 'Aye Biwi, She is fine. She had just fallen asleep.'

Allah finally ended our confinement in that verandah on the same day. One night when Dadi Amma fell silent, she never spoke again. Preparations began to be made for her last rites and I was given a holiday. What a happy day it was. The next day was even better. Our father came and we learnt that he would take us back with him.

Happy, we accompanied him to Jhansi. My father lived there in a large bungalow. Abba had kept it very well. He had also brought with him several older maids who had worked for the family. He had thought of everything and had even brought a new mother for us. This was our late Manjhli Amma. There was an army of men and women working for us. There was constant hustle and bustle in the house. Two tutors, one for English and the other for Urdu, were appointed for me. I was so afraid of the Urdu tutor that I would lose my voice in his presence and for an hour he would repeat the lessons while I listened. Two more years passed thus.

In these two years I learnt a lot—how to ride goats, how to tie a canister to the tail of a cow before making her run, finding bird nests in the bushes, climbing trees and challenging the European and Anglo-Indian children living in neighbouring bungalows to stone-pelting. I also grew acquainted with the geography of the land within a radius of four miles, becoming familiar with every hillock, every ruin, every tree, every bush and every rock in that area.

I learnt all this very rapidly before I was sent off as a boarder to the Islamic High School in Etawah. People there must have presumed that no one had cared for me or taught me anything. This was absolutely untrue. After my mother's death, Allah gave me another extremely loving mother. It was she who was also my teacher. What she taught me still flows in each vein of mine. This was Ashfaq Jahan, my sister who was a year older than I and whom I call Achhu Baji (may God give her a long life). She was a special person. I was taller and better built than her. When angry, I would push her. I would bite or pinch her but she would continue to smile. At night, when I would see the bruises I had left on her fair arms, I would feel ashamed and weep. She would continue to smile while she patted me to sleep, telling me that I would grow up and make the family proud. She would talk about great things and find all sorts of tales to tell me. She never preached to me as an elder or forbade me from doing anything. What this young girl did and said left a deep impression on me and created a pride in me for my religion, my nation and the honour of my family. Because of what she told me, I came to believe that the world was full of low people among whom a few respectable people lived. Among these respectable people, I believed, our family was the most respectable. I have no idea why but Achhu Baji insisted that we were actually Arabs and that our ancestors had been great emperors. So, even though our family had lost its dominion and was living in reduced circumstances, what did it matter? After all we were from extremely respectable stock. It was only this part of her teaching that left a mark on my mind. In every other way I remained uneducated. God help me, even at the age of thirteen I did not know the English alphabet. I do not know why but I could never remember it. I did, however, recognize some letters and even knew a few words of English. Even though I did not recognize the Urdu alphabet, I had memorized two books. This was the beginning.

At thirteen, when I was as tall as a sixteen year old, my family moved to Etawah. Because of the neglect in the boarding school, my lack of intelligence, my fear of books and my overpowering pride in my family, my state was not just pitiable but also astonishing. When I returned home from school after the first year, I had neither a trunk for my belongings nor clothes, books or bedding. My hair long and my clothes filthy, I returned with a ghostly look. For weeks my family reproached me and at night my sister would hug me and weep. In the morning, she would rub my face hard with a scrubber and complain, 'Hai Hai, *my brother has become dark.' My complexion was fair and after it had gone through the ministrations of the scrubber, it would turn beetroot red. Even then Achhu Baji wasn't satisfied. Eventually, I reverted to my old habits—pushing and pinching her.*

I studied in Etawah for two years. My family then moved to Aligarh. We lived in the incomplete Jafar Manzil for some time. Then the family moved again. I was admitted to the Zahoor Ward.[9] *I do not know how I ended up in the fourth class. I now became interested in my studies, worked hard for three years and scored well in my exams. In the third year, I was appointed the* Head Monitor. *In those days the* Head Monitor *behaved like a self-willed dictator. Or at least that's how I behaved. The four junior monitors were like my ministers and I the undisputed ruler. I laid down the law. For instance, I would order that all the marrow-filled bones in*

[9] The Mohammedan Anglo Oriental Collegiate School, Aligarh, founded by Syed Ahmad Khan in 1875. It came to be popularly known as Minto Circle after the Earl of Minto (1845–1914), the Viceroy of India. Originally the primary section of the school was housed in a building known as the Zahoor Ward.

the qorma on a particular day had to be saved for me. On another day, I would order all the boys to appear in the field barefoot to play kabaddi. *In short, whatever I wished was law and no-one had the courage to defy it. I ruled for a year and then after I had appointed my own successor as well as successors of the assistant monitors, I bade a sad farewell to Zahoor Ward and moved to MacDonald House.*[10] *In Zahoor Ward I was a giant among the little boys while in MacDonald House I became an appendage to the older boys. My self-esteem was severely dented. I got drawn into group rivalries and fights. Nothing seemed to help. What did happen, however, was that I failed in the seventh class. In the meantime, my father had retired and got re-employed as assistant engineer in the princely state of Bhopal. Achhu Baji had gotten married. My younger sister, along with my stepmother, joined my father in Bhopal where I too was admitted in the eighth class. I stayed here for two years and managed to clear classes eight and nine only by threatening my teachers.*

In Bhopal I met a special person who was to leave a deep mark not only on my mind but also on my career. A tutor had been hired to teach my nephew Faruq. (I have not mentioned this but we were two brothers and four sisters. Most of them were much older than me. My oldest brother is eighteen years older than me and even today we stay miles away from each other.) The name of the tutor was Huzur Ahmad. Whenever I saw him he was either reading or muttering to himself. He always appeared pleased and even smiled when he was reading. He seemed to find something amusing about everything. He must have been around thirty. I disliked him from the moment I saw him and therefore ignored him and it was six months before I was forced to speak to him. Then we spoke again and thus, accidentally, I discovered that he was a magnet towards whom I was drawn. He did not know a word of English and could barely manage to read books in Arabic. But his knowledge of Urdu and Persian was another

[10] The name of the building housing the secondary section of the school. It is one of the hostels of a hall of residence known as the Aftab Hall.

matter. He was like a walking library. He had a great interest in history. His taste in literature was highly developed. He was a poet and wrote under the pen name Huzur. He wrote very little and the little that he wrote, he destroyed. He used to say that he was still learning and would start writing formally when he was forty.

Huzur Ahmad opened up a new world for me. I had been totally ignorant till then but now I began to look at learning differently. I was already quite old but what could I have done? Either I had been given no memory or it had been sacrificed while I was a child to relatives who believed learning meant memorizing by rote. The Urdu journal Makhzan *had just begun publishing with much fanfare. I tried reading it and after struggling for an hour managed to read only a page; instead of enjoying it, I ended up being totally distracted. There was nothing to do but to pick Huzur Ahmad's brain which I constantly did but I was never satisfied nor did he tire of me. We would sit beside the Motia Lake and carry on a one-sided conversation. He would do the talking and I would listen. 'Look, Rafiq Miyan, how simply Hafiz expresses this idea.' He would recite a couplet of the great Persian poet and tell me the meaning of each word. Then he would explain the couplet. He would touch upon all the finer points of the poetry. Sometimes, he would get exasperated at my ignorance of the language and say, 'Rafiq Miyan, Persian is like a handmaiden in your household. There is not a word of it that is not used in their daily speech by the people of Lucknow....'*

In a year I began to understand and speak Persian (though not read it because until today I cannot read Urdu well). This pleased him. In his opinion, what was obvious was useless. The hidden was what was real and that is how it should be. What a man was able to master was his most valuable possession.

It was a pity that my association with Huzur Ahmad ended soon after. In two years we too left Bhopal for Etawah where father had decided to settle down. In 1918 Huzur Ahmad passed away with his poetic ambitions unfulfilled, but I had been deeply affected by him. I wanted to acquire profound learning but had no clue as to why and what I was to study. I hated all the subjects they taught at school. I didn't know Urdu, Persian or English. History and Geography had been invented by idiots for idiots. I did, however, develop an interest in mathematics. I concentrated on arithmetic. And when I began to pay attention to it, my interest bloomed and I began to enjoy myself. In a week I had solved Chakravarti's textbook.[11] *Enthusiastically, I went to my teacher and even approached the headmaster to prescribe a more advanced book for me, but in vain. I discovered that I was supposed to learn this much and no more in one year. I was very disappointed. I then took up Geometry. Like a novel I devoured it. When I had finished the prescribed book, I turned to Algebra. I not only solved the problems in the book in a month but in the process also learnt English. We stayed in Etawah for only ten months. Azim Beg Chughtai*[12] *was a classmate and was one of my four good friends. Udham Usman was another and I forget the name of the third whom we called the leather spade. They called me Mowgli (after the boy who was brought up by wolves in Kipling's* Jungle Book*). We were all wild. Eventually I ran away from home. With a bundle of books of mathematics (unfortunately all of them borrowed) and two sets of clothes I reached Bombay. I wanted to become an engineer. For a fortnight I searched in vain for a job. Eventually, I was hired as a coolie in Napier Foundry and Engineering Works. Here, the coolies were made to work for only twelve hours a day. From six in the morning to noon and from one in the afternoon to seven in the evening, I would carry iron.*

[11] Professor Jadav Chandra Chakravarti was a Professor of Mathematics at Aligarh Muslim University which he had joined in 1888. He authored an extremely popular textbook of mathematics which was used for over a century and was translated into many Indian and European languages.

[12] 1895–1941, Prolific writer of humour, historical essays and short stories. Author of *Koltaar, Sharir Biwi* and *Khurpa Bahadur*. Also older brother and early mentor of Ismat Chughtai.

Jet-black with dirt, hands unwashed (because washing them would have meant wasting time) I would eat at wayside eateries and go to bed immediately. I would then get up at two in the morning and study till five, preparing for the entrance exam to the VIT Institute. The Institute demanded average competence in English and Mathematics. I also needed to study a bit of Chemistry and Physics both of which were new for me. I was also very nervous about English. Lord knows what else I studied. In the factory I was promoted and I began to earn a rupee and a quarter a day. There was little to spend it on so I bought twenty to thirty books from the Chor Bazaar and read them. For six months things carried on thus. I wrote the exam, passed and was admitted to the Institute. I now informed my family of my whereabouts. The first congratulatory telegram and money order I received from Achhu Baji. Her letter followed. Finally, I had joined the mainstream again. I became a student and began to live like a human being again. Unfortunately, my intelligence and the fickleness of my temperament had ruined me. In every department of the engineering college there were books and I was enthusiastic about that. God had gifted me with intellect (though with no memory) so I went through all the books prescribed for the first year. Then I read the books prescribed for the second, third and fourth years (which even included mathematics prescribed for BSc). Now, with nothing more to read, what was I to do since I had read all that was necessary for an engineering degree? For the next three years I did not buy or read any book related to my subjects at the Institute. In my arrogance I would pick arguments with my professors. I would skip classes and squander my time. There was no one to guide me as to what to read in literature. I would buy second-hand novels and read them. On a visit to Lucknow during my vacation in Nakkhas I saw a book called The Martyrdom of Man *and bought it.*[13] *(Unfortunately I lost it and never*

[13] *The Martyrdom of Man*, published in 1872, presented a secular view of history which was as revolutionary as Darwin's view of science; it influenced many thinkers including H.G.Wells and George Orwell.

found it again.) It was written by the nephew of Charles Grey, Edward Charles.[14] *The book was thick, nearly five hundred pages, and I read it at least a dozen times. The author wanted to write a history of the world but it ended up being about the grandeur of the human mind. This book affected me profoundly. People believed it had turned me into an atheist. Whatever the truth, it was a fact that in three years I only read that one book. In 1920, I appeared for my final exams. They finished on a Saturday and on Monday I found a job in an engineering company. I worked for two months and then ran home. In 1917, I had gotten married hence I couldn't afford to stay unemployed. Now when I looked for a job again, I couldn't find one. Finally, I managed to get into the railway workshop in Jhansi. I worked there for six months before I quit. Work on the Sharda canal began and I found my next job working on it and was based in the jungles at Ban Basa. I worked there for nine months before I returned home. In November 1921, I was summoned again to work on the Sharda project and was then posted in Shahgarh. During this stint I fought with my superior officers, Mr Shelly and Mr Roach, and kept threatening to resign till they were themselves transferred and the rest of my life was ruined forever.*

The short, rotund Rai Sahib Lala Ram Narain and Anand Prakash replaced them as assistant engineer and executive engineer, respectively. Initially, there were skirmishes with the new officers too but both of them appreciated efficiency. One took on the role of my mother and the other of my father and together they anointed me as their favourite child. For six years life passed as a celebration. There were cards to play and animals to hunt. There were no rules or restrictions. Yet I remained devoted to my work. When needed, I was ready to stake my life for it and stayed on top of things. I did much more than was expected of me. However, my contempt for deadlines, rules and subordination continued. My temperament continued to be wild and my arrogance grew. I developed a

[14] His memory seems to have failed him here. The author of the book was William Winwood Reade.

liking for leisure. I did not read a single book during this time. This period of pleasure too ended. Officers started to be transferred. The very idea of working under anyone other than Anand Prakash and Ram Narain was unimaginable. I resigned but my resignation was not accepted. I escaped. Then began an unparalleled spell of wanderings. Since then I have had fourteen jobs. Everywhere they were happy with my work. I left Sagauli four times, Karera thrice. The manager and general manager sent someone to my house to persuade me to rejoin. They tried everything to convince me. But alas, I had got used to the pampering of Anand Prakash Sahib and Ram Narain Sahib. I will never find patrons like them nor will I stay long at any job. These days I am the planning superintendent in the Government Central Workshop in Kanpur. I have often tried to quit but have not been allowed to. If I decide to quit without permission I will be arrested and dragged back under the Ordinance Act. I languish here and bewail my fate.

This is the long story of my short life.

I am a small man, I am true, I am mad, I am crazy. Whatever I am, here I am.

According to those who remembered him, Rafiq Hussain was over six feet tall, lean, in fact almost skeletal, wide-boned, very fair, with a wide forehead and a prominent nose. His hair was thick and shaggy and his eyes distracted and restless. A loner by nature, he did not like company and his eccentricities made the old crones in his family refer to him as crazy. He was a chain-smoker and was not very particular about which brand of cigarettes or *bidis* he smoked. Towards the end of his life he was smoking raw tobacco without the intervening filter or a tile from a *chillum*. He drank countless cups of tea.

He had a violent temper and a short fuse. He was also an

extremely kind and generous man who painted and taught children tricks. As an engineer he was very hardworking and equally demanding of those who worked under him. He taught the coolies who worked for him not only how to sign their names but also mentored them into eventually becoming technicians and overseers themselves.

He came from a family of two brothers and three sisters. His mother died when he was very young and even though he says that his father's second marriage settled things, discord seems to have continued. It was to escape his stepmother's taunts of being good for nothing that he left home without telling anyone and this was the reason why he did not let his family know where he was until he secured admission in an engineering college.

He had a close relationship with his sisters. His niece Altaf Fatima recalls asking her mother about her relationship with her brother. She was told, 'You have no idea, child! Children who have lost their mother cannot bear to see each other unhappy, particularly the girls who start playing mother to their brothers, even if they are younger than him.'

He was married twice; once while he was still studying. His first wife Saira died at childbirth leaving two infants, Sultan and Qamar. He then married Musharraf, the daughter of a cousin and had one more son, Usman. Altaf Fatima hints that his second wife was unhappy with his tendency to frequently quit jobs. She also recalls a more telling incident. His wife visited Lahore after he died and asked to see the Shalimar Gardens. Fatima recalls how carefully she looked at each stone and corner, how she felt the carvings with her hands, how she was enthralled by the *baradari* and the canals and seemed lost to the world while she was there. Later, when Fatima commented on this, her aunt said, 'What can I say daughter? It's a gift from your uncle. He has systematically educated me. When he showed me the Taj Mahal, the Red Fort, the Chittorgarh fort, the ruins and temples of Ajmer and Rajputana, he made me familiar with each brick and made those times come alive again. He took me into every canopy. He seemed to shake me awake, "Aye Begum, look at this! All this is your past. Internalize it, Begum. Immerse yourself in it".'

His relatives have described how his stories were created and how he worked with his silent collaborators—his younger sister Sayyida Mumtaz and his daughter Qamar, the two who according to him, were the ones who had started him writing in Urdu. Their challenging him and their assistance to him in creating these stories needs to be acknowledged. His daughter was his assistant. Rafiq Hussain is supposed to have made holes in the paper on which he wrote and he admits his handwriting was so illegible that he himself had difficulty reading it. He made many spelling mistakes too. Qamar would copy out his drafts for him to work on them further. It has been suggested that he could not have written his stories without her help.

He would make an outline of a story in a mixture of Urdu and English. His daughter would help turn it into elegant prose by finding words to replace the English phrases. Qamar also had a beautiful handwriting.

His niece Altaf recalls what his writing meant to them:

'Those stories of his were a nuisance for us. The day he entered the house carrying papers with his unformed handwriting on it, we knew that we would have be quiet and be on a speech-fast.

Both sister and brother accorded to the reading and listening of short stories almost the status of worship. *Amma* (mother) would keep away her *paans*, areca nut cracker, the stitching or embroidery that she was currently doing and indicate to us to leave them alone. She would rearrange her dupatta and settle down. She would then listen carefully to every word. Sometimes they would stop and discuss the writing. A word would be added or another deleted. On one of these days even the crows would fly away and not caw.

I remember the day he brought his short story *"Aina e Hairat"*. My aunt came with him. After a round of tea, silence was ordered. He was in a strange state that day. Even today the heavy, resounding and sombre voice echoes in my ears, "Listen Sheila! Listen Firdaus Bano! O Abdul Hakim listen! Tick, tick, tick!" When he reached this point, his voice cracked for he had begun to cry. My mother's eyes too had begun to water and my aunt sat in silence.'

Between him, his sister and daughter there was a special bond; they also played an intellectual game between themselves where each had to tell a tale which made an assigned impossible situation probable.

While he was working on the Sharda canal he was stationed in the densely forested area in the *Terai* and it is then that he became interested in *shikar*. Syed Akbar, a nephew, recalls Rafiq Hussain telling him that he would replace the tyres and tubes on his bicycle wheels with thick ropes so that he would not have to worry about punctures and could roam hilly terrain to hunt deer and rabbits. Often, if it got late, he would spend the night in the forest on some tree. He made friends with a local landlord called Haji Abdul Hamid who was an avid hunter. Abdul Hamid used to organize elaborate tiger hunts, almost like royal hunts. He invited guests and scores of attendants looked after everyone's needs. Rafiq Hussain seems to have begun hunting big game under his influence. But he couldn't afford *machans* and other equipment when he went into the jungle himself, so he often spent the night on the branch of a tree, waiting for a tiger to come back to feed on an earlier kill or simply observing the jungle at night.

He had a very brief writing career. He probably wrote his first piece called 'Ummeed' (Hope) in 1937–38 but 'Kaffara' (Atonement) was published first. This was followed by 'Kalwa', 'Biru', 'Shirin-Farhad', '*Aina e Hairat*' (The Mirror of Wonders) and 'Gori ho Gori'. All his writing was done within the span of a decade and he only wrote when he was unemployed. He never accepted any money for his writings.

He died of cancer. His first collection of stories *Aina e Hairat* was published a fortnight after he died in 1944.

Atonement

If you disembark at the Shahgarh railway station and head north across five villages, you reach the last village, Sukhdaspur. Beyond the village is a vast rolling expanse of land. More than two miles wide, it spreads up to where the horizon is blocked by a dark, greenish wall which begins on the right from the high banks of the Sharda canal and as it stretches to the left it gets dimmer until it disappears from sight. This is no wall but a part of the *Terai* forest known as the Muzaffarabad Range. Since the forest is full of herbivores, nothing can be grown in the vast field adjoining it except one crop of wheat. And that too became possible only after all the people living in the villages bordering the forest agreed to build a wall of thorny branches along the seemingly endless length of the forest. This protects the crop to some extent. Actually, the field which is more than ten miles long and over two miles wide, when covered by a wheat crop, seems to protect itself; for in a field as large as this, it is not easy to notice any damage done. At eight in the night, various groups of sambar[1] and *chital*,[2] with their wide-branched antlers and flared nostrils, pick open a spot in the thorny

[1] The sambar is the largest of the deer family. Even though it is also referred to as *barasingha* or 'the one with twelve antlers,' it has only eight, four on one branch and four on the other. Its coat is mud coloured. (Author)

[2] *Chital* is smaller than the sambar. The male has twelve tined antlers. Its reddish brown coat has white spots outlined in black. (Author)

fortification with their mouths, then with their wide antlers make this opening wider than their bodies, and enter the field. All night they feed freely, and as the first faint rays of the sun appear, they make their way out through the same passages and disappear into the forest.

Five days have passed since the fire of Holi was lit and it is two o'clock on a moonlit night. Close to the thorny barricade, six *chital* hinds have been feeding for hours on the knee-high wheat crop. They casually pick leaves off the drying wheat plants. At a spot closer to the edge of the field is a clump of wheat plants, a foot or two high, still green. Three *chital* hinds stay close to it. Near them, but outside the field stands a handsome *chital* buck,[3] his muscular neck arched, wearing his handsome antlers like a crown. He is silent, lost in thought. His limbs, head, eyes are all still. Only his ears turn in different directions from time to time. His vision is not powerful enough to pierce the darkness of the dense forest. The wind, too, is against him for it is blowing from the field towards the forest and thus carries no useful smells. He is, thus, dependent only on his ears. Far in the dense forest, from time to time, there is a slight rustling sound and from his right he can hear a faint knocking. He is not in the least concerned about either of these two sounds. The first he recognizes as the sounds of baby mongooses playing among dry leaves and the second is the blue nuthatch pecking at the bark of trees, looking for bugs. The stag is concerned about the slight movement of a long creature crouching close to the ground among the *sal* trees that he detected a short while ago. Is it a tiger or something else? Just that one faint sound of the crackling of a dry leaf crushed by a paw is enough to alert him.

However, it seems unbelievable that a tiger will step carelessly on a dry leaf. Even though the ground was covered with dry *sal*

[3] Female *chital* are called *chitlin* and male ones *jhanak*. (Author)

leaves the two tigers approached without making any sound and sat down behind a small anthill waiting for the herd to return. Between them and the hinds were many clumps of *bhat*[4] and *maror phali*[5] and they too could not see a thing but that did not worry them as they crouched there. The strong wind blowing from the field to the forest carried with it the scent of the *chital* and the sounds of their grazing.

Suddenly, the tigress detects a new scent in the wind and, worried, she turns her head. The tiger has not perceived the new smell and he continues to sit motionlessly until another gust of strong wind reaches them. Now he too smells the new scent. Irritated, he bends both ears forward but the worried tigress stands up. Another gust of wind blows their way and there is no longer any doubt. The pair stands up, turns around and starts moving slowly from the north towards the east.

In the field outside the forest the stag still stands as he was. Instead of three, now five hinds gambol around the green clump of wheat. The other four continue to feed on the leaves of the drying wheat crop but soon these four also pick up the new scent and, one by one, stop feeding and lift their heads. One of them looks toward the stag who still stands indifferently, trying to pick up sounds from the forest. One hind spots a faint movement in the direction of Sukhdaspur and she immediately makes a long *koo* sound. This sound from the edge of the forest echoes in the quiet night and alerts all the other *chital* who stop feeding and stand still with their heads lifted. The stag too turns around. For five minutes all these animals stand as motionless as stone carvings. The scent is still there but there is no movement now. Five minutes later, the thing in the distance moves again. All the *chital* immediately leap

[4] A wild grass with large leaves. It is 12–18 inches high. (Author)

[5] Wild hemp. It grows like sticks and is four to five feet high. (Author)

towards the forest. One by one, they leap through a breach in the thorny barricade and bound away into the forest. Finally the stag joins the queue formed by the does at the breach. Before entering the forest, the same hind who had called out earlier calls twice more—*koo, koo*—and all the *chital* disappear into the forest. Some distance away, in the wheat field, stands a worried man.

To escape inevitable death at the gallows, Bihari, crazed by fear, had avoided the village and headed straight to the forest from Shahgarh railway station.

In his mind, the dense forest, laden with flowers and fruit and watered by small springs waited with open arms to hide him in its depths. Now, close to it, he began to fear the forest too. Behind him, the flickering lights in the village seemed like the eyes of death. In front of him was the forest which until now he had sought as a womb, but which now appeared dark and frightening as a grave. He had seen or smelt nothing. All he had heard were the three calls of the *chital* hind and these calls changed his imaginary paradise into a terrifying, impenetrable jungle. Bihari had grown up in a village and knew the fear of ghosts and malignant spirits but he was completely unfamiliar with jungles. His heart began to pound for he felt himself surrounded by death and grew faint. He sat down there in the field, put his head in his hands and began to weep at his own helplessness. In his mind was such a tumult of thoughts that he could not concentrate on any one for long. Sometimes, he thought of his own ill fortune and sometimes of his old parents. At times he tried to take stock of his predicament and draw up a plan for his future. However, no matter what he thought about, one image superimposed itself: a moonlit night, the mound-like boundary of a field, a man soaked in blood, sprawled head downwards, and him standing at the man's feet, chopper in hand. Bihari shivered and shuddered at the image. He tried hard to banish it but it kept returning. He told himself repeatedly, 'Hey Ram, it is true that I am the murderer of Baldev Singh? How, how on earth, did this happen? Yes, I hit him with the chopper. I hit him gently on the head twice but the third time I struck him hard and caught him in the stomach. Did he collapse because of this wound to his stomach? No, how did the stomach wound matter? The first strike with the chopper had already opened his skull. Did I kill him? What happened? *Hey* Ram! What happened? *Hey* Ram! What's happening? Oh God, can he come back to life? No! No! Oh *Bhagwan*! Will I be forgiven? No! No....'

As these thoughts swamped his mind, the cool breeze carrying gentle waves of sleep, presented his tired brain with a strange new image. He saw Baldev Singh standing with his father in front of him, and the father telling the son, 'Kunwar Bhaiyya, see here's Bihari in front of you. Forgive him now. You'll feel better.' Blood dripped from Baldev Singh's mouth as he stood there with his eyes shut. Occasionally he would open his eyes slightly, look at him and then close them again. His father held him with both hands while constantly pleading, 'Now Kunwar, let it go. Forgive him. You'll recover.' Then the old man turned to him and spoke angrily, 'Bihari, why don't you ask for forgiveness? What are you staring at? Ask for mercy.' Bihari, with folded hands, asks to be forgiven. Baldev Singh shakes his head and says to his father, 'I won't forgive him.' Bihari falls at his feet, to which Baldev Singh says, 'I will not forgive. Call the police. Arrest him! Catch him! Catch him! Run! Come on, help catch him!"'

Bihari woke up and imagined scores of men racing towards him. With a start, he got to his feet. The pleasant light of dawn seemed scary. The golden-yellow field of wheat seemed like an illusion erased by death. The black jungle's edge appeared like the wall of a fort in which he could find refuge from death. He sprang towards it but stopped a few paces later, and looked back to see if anyone was pursuing him. Peering from behind a tree he saw the houses of Sukhdaspur. Each house looked at him dubiously. Bihari ran to the jungle, jumped through the thorny fortification and disappeared.

He opened his eyes the second time the cock crowed. The faint light of dawn was spreading. Close by, on some tree, a peacock flapped his wings after a night of folding them close to himself. Above his head on a branch, a small bird chirped *cheen choon, cheen choon*. With each moment, along with the light, the bird's twittering grew louder. Bihari moved his limbs that had been crouched for days and felt pain in every joint. He sat up muttering, '*Hey Bhagwan*, have mercy, *Bhagwan*,' and slowly opened the rope with which he had tied his chest and waist to two branches of the banyan tree so that he would not fall over while asleep. Eight days had passed since Bihari had entered the forest. He had woven a rope out of hemp. At night he gathered ears of wheat from the field, roasted them the way chick peas are roasted in their pods, and ate them. Then he would climb up some sturdy tree at the edge of the forest and tie himself to its branches to sleep.

As soon as the day broke he went into the jungle and hid in the enclosed clearing (*chandar*) there. He found that nothing he had imagined about the forest was true. The jungle of *sal* was actually like a field in which among plants of *bhitar* and *kiryari* a foot or so high, stood lakhs of straight, naked, branchless trunks. Fifty or sixty feet above, a few branches held up a canopy-like roof of leaves. It was impossible to climb up these trees to spend the night on them or to walk among them during the day. At eight or nine in the morning, flocks of cows and buffaloes with their herders entered the forest. Closer to the cultivated fields, however, were trees with low, spreading branches. There were also dense clusters of bushes of various sizes but it was neither possible nor safe to hide in them during the day. The *sal* forest spread for miles northwards. To its east flowed the Hardoi branch of the Sharda canal and in the west, next to the impenetrable forest of *acacia catecu,* was the clearing. In the middle of this *chandar* was a small ditch or lake, on the edges of which, crouching or standing in the mire and the swamp, Bihari spent the day. Leeches clung to his legs, arms and back and countless insects buzzed around his face. The *chandar* was a patch of land where innumerable varieties of reeds and grasses grew, unrestrained and high. It was nearly impossible for a human being to step into these and hope to find a place to put his foot on the ground. The grass was high enough to hide an elephant along with its howdah. Not a single tree in a *chandar* is high enough for a man to climb to a perch six or seven feet above the ground. It is also impossible to crush the stalks of grass to flatten out a small patch even two feet square for the grass is so hard that it cannot be cut except with a sharp instrument. And now the season has changed. Holi is over. The green, swaying *chandar* is dry and dead after four months of harsh cold. Birds do not twitter here any longer, nor can one hear the black partridge call. The rustling brown *chandar* now waits for the spark that inevitably manages to reach all *chandars* and forces the grass into fiery extinction. When the *chandar* emerges again, covered in brown-black ashes, another generation of plants push their heads through the ash on this cremation ground, smiling. Cruel, cruel—how cruel are the laws of nature!

The *chandar* begins to grow again. New beings, never in search of life themselves, are unconsciously brought into existence and left to survive the hot and cold gusts of wind. Life is short and has its afflictions. The harsh seasons and the struggle for life continue unabated and life goes on until it ends the same way. Cruel, cruel—how cruel are the laws of nature! Large trees, small plants, countless varieties of grass, large beasts, smaller quadrupeds, birds, little animals, and crores of insects and humans: all continue to be born because of these laws. The wheels of the mill keep turning. Grain is fed into it and flour emerges. Perhaps, the divine plan is itself atonement for some great sin.

For long stretches of time, Bihari, rope in one hand, picking at the bark of the banyan with the other, would sit on his perch in the banyan, thinking. He felt so wretched at the turn his life had taken that he almost decided to go into one of the nearby villages and try to pass as a *sadhu* or a *faqir.* He was even prepared to be hanged if caught, for his sufferings seemed unbearable. He had nothing with him except a matchbox and some useless rupees. He wished he had at least a pen-knife. The matchsticks were about to run out. At the thought of the matchbox, he took it out of the pocket of his torn coat. Counting the sticks left, he carefully put it back in his pocket and muttering, '*Bhagwan, O Bhagwan*, have mercy!' he began to climb down from his perch. When he reached the last branch, he held it with both hands and swung from it. His feet were about four feet above the ground when he released his grip and landed with a thud. He could not keep his balance and sat there, hands on the ground. At this very moment, from sixty feet to his right he heard a woman scream, '*Arey Daiyya*, O mother!' He turned to look and saw a woman, who had been relieving herself, leave her vessel of water behind, and run away. Bihari too panicked and ran into the forest. Suddenly he thought of the *lota* the woman had left behind. He ran to get it. When he went to pick it up he saw a large bundle wrapped in cloth. He took that too and with the water dripping from the *lota* he ran in the opposite direction from the way the woman had gone. Weakened by his hunger and his struggles, he soon began to pant. He stopped running and with large strides entered the *chandar*.

In the *chandar* Bihari opened the bundle and found a spade, a sickle, two ounces of tobacco, a *chillum*, a matchbox, *rotis* made of a seer and a quarter of flour, and cooked brinjals. Using the spade and the sickle, Bihari immediately cleared a space in a dry part of the *chandar*. He then fetched some water in the *lota*. He had been in the jungle for eight days and he relished this meal. He lit a fire, readied the *chillum* and smoked at leisure. The food and tobacco intoxicated him and he went off to sleep right there. He fell asleep at ten in the morning and slept till four in the afternoon. How can one ever sleep well on a tree?

Once awake, for no apparent reason, he felt cheerful. Earlier in the day, he had felt depressed and decided to go back to the villages. Now he felt differently. The urge to live had reawakened. Looking at the sickle, it struck him that the wheat harvest must have begun. Immediately, he grew eager to collect as much of it from the fields as he could and hide it in the forest; for once the wheat was harvested, what would he eat? He no longer had the courage to return to human habitations for he was certain that he would be caught the moment he was amongst people. He decided he would stay hidden in the forest as long as he could. He had eaten a full meal after days and his spirits were rekindled.

As soon as it was evening, he emerged from the *chandar* and began walking along the 'hundred-foot road,'[6] planning his future,

[6] The Department of Forests has constructed these roads in all the jungles of Awadh. Some of them are motorable but most are overgrown by bushes. These roads help stop forest fires from spreading and also help to map out the jungles. (Author)

when his eyes fell on the left side of the road. There, he saw a tiger approaching him. Sweating, he froze where he stood. Bihari had begun to believe there were no tigers or wolves in these jungles. Now, for the first time, he saw a tiger. However, the tiger had seen him twice before and now, on the third occasion, they were face to face. The tiger turned his large, royal head majestically, looked behind him for a moment and then continued to walk very slowly, looking at him calmly and grandly. As if in a trance, Bihari watched as he saw another tiger approach at a faster gait. This was the tigress. She was nearing the end of her pregnancy and was irritable. As soon as she reached her mate, she saw Bihari and a slight growl escaped her. The male tiger slowed down. As soon as the tigress came up beside him on his left, the tiger turned toward the forest, nudging the angry tigress, and led her away with him.

Bihari was so petrified that even after the tigers had disappeared into the forest, he continued to stand still. He did not know which way to head or what to do. He finally began to walk, but had not gone far when he heard a peacock shriek behind him. He looked back and saw that the tigers, after taking a detour through the jungle, had reemerged on the road and were walking away from him. The tigers were annoyed by Bihari's constant presence in the jungle but the male tiger was wise and of calm temperament. He had realized that matters were getting volatile. His empress was pregnant and was in urgent need of peace and quiet. Because of this human's presence, the few hog deer and barking deer which had lived in the area had moved away. Even the herds of sambar and *chital* which used to pass this way had stopped doing so. There was starting to be a shortage of food. It would be better to move to the bulrushes beside the Chuka river, and that is where he headed with the tigress. After an easy walk of four kilometres, they reached the main Sharda canal. In front of them was the bridge over the Chuka Dhaiyya but they did not need it. Two hundred paces before it, they drank from the Sharda canal and then swam across.

Bihari had been busy till very late in the wheat field and when he woke up the sun was up. Alarmed, he looked around, and was horrified to see three or four red turbans in the distance. Hurriedly, he unfastened himself and descended from the tree. The base of the tree was completely surrounded by dense *corinda* bushes and a creeper covering them. He crouched amongst these bushes and out of fear stopped breathing freely. However, he could not do anything about his heart which sounded like a drum beat. As the voices of the police and other men drew nearer, he even closed his eyes and muttered, 'Hey Ram, I'm all alone and the whole world is against me. What sins have I committed? And in which life?' The vision of that moonlit night reappeared in his mind's eye—how the chopper had first scraped Baldev Singh's head as it entered his skull. His right hand had felt the jolt as the chopper's sharp blade cut through live bone. His mind took a twist and erased the thought and for some reason he began arguing with himself.

'No doubt I am a criminal, but I do not deserve punishment. I would never have done what I did if my friends had not got me drunk and if Baldev Singh's father had not been so cruel to me. He deprived me of my rights and appropriated my land, my orchard... but as retaliation...to kill his son? Murder! Murder?...Murder? Yes, murder! I was drunk and in that state Ramzani incited me.... Jamuna is my fiancée...she is my fiancée. Baldev was in her house too... Jamuna!...Jamuna? Whose is she now? *Hey* Ram, have mercy....'

The men's voices were very close now and they were heading his way. He heard Khan, the senior police *darogha*, 'You've gone crazy. Do dacoits harvest fields? Do they steal wheat? If there's a dacoit, there would have been an incident somewhere.'

A voice, 'Sir, he's alone. There's no one else with him.'

The senior *darogha* said, 'Right, you idiot. Single dacoits do commit crimes, but they rob lone travellers. They enter houses when people sleep. Do they go around stealing wheat? And a stupid dacoit who does not even have a pen-knife! Didn't you say he picked the wheat with his hands at first? Did you check that carefully? Can you tell from the stubs if the wheat has been picked by hand?'

A voice, '*Arey* sir! I can tell by just looking at the stubs which have been eaten by animals and which have been cut with a sickle. Sir, this one is a dangerous criminal.'

The senior *darogha*, 'Then he's an absolutely new criminal. Clearly, he has run away after killing someone. He must be that murderer on the run—what was his name? Do you remember? Did you read that circular?'

The heavy voice of a police constable, 'Bihari, son of Mahabir of Makrawan. The victim: Baldev Singh.'

A voice, 'We won't find him here. He must be in the *chandar* or in the *catechu acacia* forest. Let's go there!'

The senior *darogha*, 'You fool, I know that. I want to look for footprints here. And do you think we'll find him if we go into the *chandar*? Even if five hundred men went looking for him they wouldn't be able to find him there. We can only catch him when he comes out. He's bound to return to some village or other soon. All of you be on the lookout. Whoever catches him or brings information about him will be well rewarded.'

Life. Life, the most valuable thing in the world! Life, you are preserved in all sorts of ways. The blind old woman beside the road sobs as she begs. Her youth, the crowd of lovers, luxuries, pleasures, wealth, family and home—all have gone. Nothing remains for her. Why then is she living? What is she waiting for? Time will not undo itself. Why then is she alive? For life! She still has her most valuable possession, life. And it is this she nurtures at a heavy price.

Farewell! O worlds of humans, farewell! Bihari is never going to head your way again.

Miles away from human habitation, the banks of the Chuka Daiyya covered in thick, green bushes and ferns, slope down to verdant, cooling bushes and then meet up with a fifteen-feet high growth of dense bulrushes. When the jungle is dry and fires rage everywhere, here you find hundreds of birds swinging on flowering branches as they sing ragas to nature. From one spot amongst these bulrushes emanates a strange odour. Here, on the moist earth, the tiger and tigress have made a home for themselves, carpeted with tender bulrushes. In this haven, protected both from cold and light, the tigress has given birth to cubs that she now looks at intently as she lies on her side. Behind her lies the tiger, fast asleep. The cubs are old enough for their eyes to have opened and they are playing with one another. Light stripes have begun to appear on their golden fur. It is dusk and the tigress is waiting for her lord to wake up so that they can go up the slope, a little further from the snake line[7] to the bushes of Rohini[8] where the remaining half of the sambar they killed yesterday lies. The tiger stretches himself, lifts his head and looks at his cubs. The tigress immediately gives a vigorous

[7] The snake line is a road that runs halfway up the slope. Since the slope is uneven, the road undulates like a snake. It is in no way similar to a real road but is just a track from which trees have been cut. (Author)

[8] A bush bearing flowers from which runs a red medicinal sap. I have no idea what it is used for but the locals collect it. (Author)

shrug and gets to her feet. The two fat brown cubs, who had been climbing over her to attack each other, tumble down to the ground and roll over.

As soon as the tiger sits up, the tigress walks out on the path that their constant comings and goings have beaten into the bulrushes. The tigress is hungry for she is feeding her cubs and her appetite has grown. Eventually, the tiger leaves too. Once out of the bulrushes, he stretches himself in a leisurely manner and casually begins to follow the tigress. As soon as they leave the cane rushes and emerge on to the snake line, a peacock perched sixty feet high on a *sakhu* (*shorea robusta*) shrieks *meeaon, meeaon*. Scores of monkeys sitting on a *haldu* tree begin to chatter. The tigers did not have to hunt today so there was no reason for them to conceal themselves. If the jungle found out about them, let it. They kept walking freely on the snake line. When they were below the Rohini cluster, they leapt, one after the other, on to the embankment, and after walking a bit among the bushes they reached the remains of the sambar carcass.

Once there, their calm royal demeanour changed into rage and indignation. The tiger grew furious. His soft and delicately swaying queen turned into an agitated bloodthirsty tigress. Meat had been stolen; there was the scent of a human. The tip of the tiger's straight tail started to quiver indicating his state of mind. The tigress was even angrier. Two sounds similar to a cobra's hiss escaped her. She sniffed at the sambar's bones and hide as she walked around it. She then left and walked away in one direction. Today, she was going to settle scores with that wretched thief. This was the third time meat from their kill had been stolen. The tiger followed but soon the constancy of his character prevailed. He began walking faster and overtook the tigress. They walked for about three furlongs and as soon as the tiger put his head out of the dense grass and looked at the open fire line he saw the running man two hundred paces away. The tiger stepped back and turned to his right, and keeping to his right he made the tigress turn around too and guided her along onto the banks of the canal.[9]

If there is anything that can create conflicting emotions in the human mind, it is the jungles of the *Terai*. Those who have not been in these jungles may not be able to conjure up their impact. If one stands on any firing line on the bank of the Chuka river slope in the evening, on both sides there are trunks of lakhs of enormous *sal* trees and if one looks up to the high roof of green leaves, the view fades into darkness till it disappears. On the slope one's view takes in hundreds of bushes covered with creepers and other delicate paddy green plants followed by bushes of green, raw, willow reed and then travels along the swaying plateau of bulrushes for miles as it fades and disappears into the forests far away. The jungle is so far away that it appears as a faint mist. There is silence all around. Sometimes a jungle fowl cackles, immediately followed by the *meeaon meeaon* of a peacock, and then silence reigns again. The scene is simultaneously enchanting and frightening. Humans feel so frightened that they want to run away immediately but also find that they do not want to leave. This is true only in the full light of day. As it gets darker, its seductiveness turns into ferocity. The heart pounds faster as the sun sets and to those who see the jungle at twilight, it looks like a terrifying ocean of death. Trees cover themselves with a blanket of darkness and assume frightening forms. At this time, the visitor yearns for light and human company. He hurriedly leaves the jungle and heads

[9] All the animals of the forest are so scared of humans that they consider it forbidden to kill them. (Author)

home. As soon as he is back with fellow human beings in the light of a lamp, his heart, on its own, thanks God.

However, in the short space of four months the desire to protect his precious life had erased such emotions from Bihari's mind. His human thoughts and emotions had become dormant. Pure animality had taken over. His face, half-hidden by the long unkempt hair of his head and beard, had begun to look different from a human's. A few strips of cloth hung from his waist to his knees. There was ferocity in his movements: his walk had the stealth of a cheetah and his eyes the alertness of deer. Now when he sat, instead of thinking of his misfortune, he concentrated on the sounds of the forest and tried to remember what they meant. Apart from roots and leaves, he began to eat bird eggs, roosting birds, dead animals and animals killed by other animals.

One morning when the peacock, as usual, created a din with his *meeaon* and the cackling of jungle fowl living among the reeds informed the jungle that the king of the jungle and his queen, after a night's outing, had returned to the bulrushes to sleep through the day and when the monkeys started to descend from the trees, Bihari too climbed down. During the night he had heard the incessant running of the sambar and the *chital* calls of *pooq pooq*. Then, from the direction of the Chuka he had heard the triumphant roar of the tiger and he knew there was a fresh kill.

His task now, before nightfall, was to find the dead beast which the tiger and tigress would have hidden with extreme care. Bihari set out to look for it but the day passed and when, disappointed, he was about to postpone his search to the next day, he suddenly noticed the drag marks of the prey. Bihari began to follow the trail. Half a mile from the bulrushes and across the snake line where the bulrushes ended, he reached the spot where a large dense tree stood in a swamp. Meat was now close by. Surely it was hidden in the tree. A crow too sat on a branch. But it was already dusk and it was dangerous to go near it. It was time for the tigers to reemerge. But Bihari had been starving for three days. He emboldened himself to go and cut off some meat from the dead animal. Splashing through the water, pushing aside the branches of the tree with both hands, he moved quickly. Just as he reached the sambar carcass covered in leaves, a peacock screamed. Jungle fowl cackled. Bihari was bent over the carcass and for a few seconds he froze, but he decided he would cut off at least one piece of meat. He got busy on the split and half-eaten carcass, cutting off a piece of meat from one spot and biting off flesh from another. He swallowed two mouthfuls and with a seer of meat in his hands, Bihari ran away from the tree and through the bushes. When he reached the snake line, there stood the tigress. A silent lightning pounced on him. The tigress, weighing four maunds, landed on the running Bihari. His waist and ribs cracked like dry reeds. Bihari lay between the front paws of the tigress like a crumpled *achkan* (long coat) that has fallen off a peg on the wall.

The tiger had been left behind and was unaware of what had happened. When he reached the spot, he stood still. The tigress held the corpse in her mouth as a cat carries a half-dead rat. She began to thrash it around. Muffled growls started emerging from his mouth. Looking at Bihari's dangling arms and dragging legs, the hair on the tiger's neck rose in fear. The tiger was not afraid of humans but watching the law of the jungle[10] being violated so

[10] People who are familiar with the jungle know the ways that tigers and elephants use to avoid humans. Once I found a recently dead sambar in a *chandar*. Its antlers were very fine. My servant and I bent down to cut off its head. From eight feet away a tiger growled and scolded us yet did not attack us. The truth is that it is much safer to move around in a jungle than it is on the streets of Delhi or Mumbai. (Author)

brazenly, he trembled. He quietly turned around and letting out sounds of *khoon, khoon, khoon, khoon*, he walked away, leaving the tigress forever. He descended and walked past the reed forests, swam across the Chuka and headed towards Nepal.

There is a strange quality in the flesh and blood of humans. Just as they say that a man goes mad when bitten by a dog, carnivores go insane once they eat human flesh. That is all they want to eat after that. This is what happened to the tigress too. After killing a forest guard and two bullock cart drivers she could find no more prey in the area of Chuka Dahiya. She, along with her cubs, crossed the canal and wandered around till she reached the jungles in the zamindari of Meenakot which adjoined cultivated lands. Here she made a succession of kills. The result was that one afternoon a circle of men drove her out of a newly grown *chandar* by creating a din. Both her young cubs were with her so she could not run far. As soon as she and the cubs emerged from the *chandar*, guns fired from the *machans* set up on the trees in front. Two shots hit her and one got a cub. Both dropped on the spot. Mahmud's bullet had hit her in the neck and Ahmad Miyan's never went astray. The second cub ran back into the *chandar* but he was caught alive with blankets.

Many years have passed since this incident. Even now a white-haired man moves around, leaning on a stick, as he deals with life's necessities, and often lowers himself with the help of his stick to sit and think of his only son, Baldev Singh. He weeps for his loss and says, '*Ay Bhagwan*, what sins did I commit to deserve this punishment?' And elsewhere, a grand, eleven-foot long tiger, sinuously moving his lean frame, paces for hours behind the bars of a cage. And when he finds no way past them, he sits down and loses himself in memories of long ago. Visitors clap, some even throw pebbles at him but he does not notice for he is deep in thought.

What could the tiger be thinking?

O Lord! For which sins is this world an atonement?

Kalua[1]

With sweat on his face, his cheeks ruddy, coat buttons undone, shirt front and fingers stained with ink, drawstring hanging to his feet, a black school bag under one arm and a black pup under the other, Munnan entered his house. His mother screamed, '*Ay hai*, I'm dead.' She stopped the humming Singer sewing machine. One hand stayed on its handle and the other went to her forehead as she watched the child. Her small smile indicated her great love. The boy turned his head to look around his small home, mimicked a heavy voice and said, '*Amman*, I am going to keep this pup.'

The mother took her hand away from her forehead. 'For God's sake, put the pup down; don't hold it so close.' Angrily, she added, 'He's soiled all your clothes. Throw him away. Your father will be returning any time now.'

The boy quickly put the pup down. The pup, wagging his three-inch tail, began to roll on the boy's shoes. The maid put her head out of the kitchen door, laughed with a finger on her nose and said to her mistress, '*Biwi*, look how the wretch rolls at his feet.' A two-year-old girl moved towards the courtyard, causing her mother to shout in exasperation. 'There she goes too. The whole house is going to be filthy. Munnan, why have you brought home this nuisance?'

Munnan said to the little girl, 'Bitto, don't come near. He'll bite.'

[1] Kalua is a derivative of Kala, meaning black.

An hour and a half later, his face washed, wearing fresh clothes, Munnan was a vision of cleanliness as he sat on the bed. The fingers of his right hand still had faint ink stains on them. In front of him in an embossed copper plate were two biscuits, three *jalebis*[2] and a cup of milk over which three flies were busy. He himself was engrossed in the pup, who was tied with a strip of cloth to the leg of a small cot near the entrance to the courtyard and was fully preoccupied with a bone. The mother raised her eyebrows and said, 'Eat! You are collecting flies! Watch it or one will fall into the milk.'

'*Amman*, he can't chew the bone. May I give him a biscuit?' The boy said as he picked up a biscuit and started to rise. The mother reacted. 'There you go to touch him again! Come on, eat it and I will....'

The lord of the house silently entered. A black cap, black-framed spectacles, black triangular beard, black *sherwani*, a black stick in his hand and black shoes on his feet. He came and stood near the small cot. His wife headed towards the kitchen with the tea pot she had picked up from the laid-out tea tray. The boy crouched where he sat, bent his head and started breaking the biscuit into his milk. The irritated master asked, 'What is this? Who brought him?'

The wife, tea pot in hand, stopped in front of the kitchen. She smiled and said, 'That nuisance just walked in the door. He was crying and his *kooonn kooonn* made me feel sorry for him. He's so sweet. I decided to tie him here.'

'*La haul!*', the husband muttered a divine deprecation and asked, 'What happens when he shits?'

'The *bhangan* will pick it up.'

'And when he urinates?'

'We'll pour water and wash it away. Come, drink your tea.'

[2] Name of a sweetmeat.

'The children will touch him.'

He got no answer because the wife was now in the kitchen. Munnan's head, however, had bent further over the cup of milk. The husband went into the room and hung everything he wore on one peg. He put on another pyjama and shirt and washed his face, vigorously rubbed his beard dry with a towel and sat down to have his tea. The wife sat close to him and began to whisk away flies. The husband spoke again, 'What filth you have collected! Have him thrown out.'

The wife got angry. 'You get obsessed by things. How is he harming us? Let him be. The children will play with him.'

'O, right! It must be this gentleman here who wants him.'

Leaving all three *jalebis*, half a biscuit and a little milk, the young gentleman went straight to the stairs and climbed up to the roof.

The black pup was a guest in the house for eight days. For two days he was in the courtyard where the husband saw the toddler touch him twice, five days in the porch where once the rope to which he was tied and once the pup itself, got tangled in the master's feet. The eighth night, the last, he had to spend on the roof. The pup missed his mother and cried loudly and the husband nudged his wife all through the night. No one slept, either on the roof or downstairs.

The next day at eleven the black pup, protesting loudly, was dragged by the maid Rahiman *bua* to the wide roads of Nakhas and entrusted to the streets. Five minutes later a motor car began growling *ghainn ghainn*. An older boy leapt and laughed and kicked him so hard that he rolled like a ball and fell into the drain. The motor car made one more sound of *ghainn* and left but the pup kept on crying *tiaanonn tiaanonn* for a long time.

There was only enough muck and water in the drain to immerse his lower half. But the drain was too deep for him and he could not get out of it. He took a few slurps of the water. Again he tried to get out by putting his front paws on the walls of the drain. Three times he cried, *kooonn*, then took his paws down and began to walk along the drain. He took eight paces before again trying unsuccessfully to get out. The rope tied to his neck dragged behind him. He kept on trying till a butcher's son saw him. He had a school bag in one hand, a writing board under his arm, a mud ink pot and a reed pen in the other. Only his feet were free. He tried to help the pup by lowering his bare foot into the drain and the pup got entirely covered in muck. In the meantime, two other sons of butchers arrived. They watched the fun for some time and then one of them bent and caught the end of the rope and with a jerk had the rope and the pup out of the drain. The dirt attached to the rope splattered. The filth caught one boy in the eye and the other tasted it as it landed inside his laughing mouth. This led to a vociferous conversation between the boys regarding the reputation of each others' mothers and sisters. The black pup lovingly looked at the boy who had pulled him out and who was now bent over, rubbing the dirt from his fingers on to the road while he matched the other boy, abuse for abuse. The pup approached him, wagging his tail. The boy looked carefully at the pup. 'He is Shera, a tiger,' he declared as he rubbed the end of the rope on the ground with his feet to clean it and then picked it up. 'Come Shera, come,' he said as he pulled at the rope. The pup took three little leaps towards him. The boy began to run. Shera kept up for a while but soon was being dragged. When his paws began to get scraped on the ground, he felt it would be better if he let himself be dragged lying down. The other two boys followed him. At the street corner sat a wrestler on a straw stool. 'You scoundrels,' he scolded the boys. 'What are you doing? Leave the pup alone.' The boys left the pup and ran away. The pup, his three-inch tail between his legs and his head to the ground, went towards the wrestler. The wrestler nudged him with his foot into the street and went back to his stool without another thought. Right there were four shops where families of *kahars*[3] lived. One of their women sat scrubbing an iron wok. The pup approached her in the same manner, head on the ground, his tail between his legs and making *kooonn kooonn* sounds. '*Dhu, dhu,*' she hushed it away.

A thin, thirteen-year-old *kahar* girl from the neighbouring shop jumped out and lifted the pup up, only to put it down immediately, muttering, 'Ram, Ram'. She rubbed both her hands on a wall to get rid of the muck and went back into the shop. She came back with water to bathe the pup. This was the pup's first bath and he hated it. He tried to run every which way. Water went into his nose and he sneezed violently a few times and was shivering by the time the bath was over. The girl dried him with a dirty piece of cloth. She crumbled some millet bread into curd and gave it to him to eat. This was the girl who gave him the name Kalua. She herself was called Chandu.

For the next two and a half months Kalua licked Chandu's hands. This period was one of great comfort. However, Bhuriya, a butcher's son who had tried to befriend Chandu but whom she had snubbed firmly a couple of times, turned hostile. One night, when every one was asleep in the street, he picked up Kalua from near her cot and ran away. First, Kalua showed his displeasure with sounds of *kooonn kooonn* and then his anger by baring his fangs but when he tried to bite, the poor creature's snout was held firmly shut. Bhuriya took him far away to one of the ancient graveyards of Bulochpur and tied him there to a jujube tree among the graves.

[3] Caste of palanquin bearers or water carriers.

Kalua spent the entire night lamenting amongst thousands of graves. In the morning, a boy wearing a *kurta* barely four inches from the ground came looking for something. When he saw Kalua, he screamed, 'Baba re! Here is the rascal.' The Baba, the *faqir* caretaker of the graveyard, appeared with a branch from a henna bush and after impolitely mentioning Kalua's sister, added, 'So it's you who screamed all night!' He began thrashing Kalua with the branch. Kalua yelped and the boy in the long *kurta* was highly amused and rolled around, laughing. Kalua, when he could no longer take the blows on his back, lay down and tried to ward off the branch with his paws. God was merciful and the branch broke.

Hungry and thirsty, Kalua stayed tied to the tree all day, thinking of Chandu. He saw no one all day, though from afar he could hear the voices of women and children, but a huge tombstone blocked his view. When it started to get dark, Kalua's nose picked up the scent of frying meat from the same direction. He could no longer keep quiet and let out a long, thin whine. A little later, when a woman approached him, he lay still from fear, his tail tucked between his legs. His tongue had been hanging out because of thirst but he quickly gathered it back and started making soft sounds of *kooonn kooonn*. The woman untied the string and led him away. Kalua followed her silently. At the other end of the graveyard were two different types of dwellings—a small room and a tomb. It was in these that the people lived.

A goat was tied nearby and four cots lay in a row. A woman and six children sat on a mat. The long-haired venerable *faqir* was sitting on his haunches on the tomb plinth, puffing *ganja*. Kalua pulled in his quivering tongue and concentrated on the smell of the *ganja*. He did not seem to like it because the tip of his nose quivered, his tongue fell out and he began panting again. The woman tied him to the peg along with the goat. As soon as the woman left, Kalua lapped up some water from the goat's earthen bowl. Infuriated by this double violation, the goat put her hooves together and threatened to attack Kalua with her sharp horns. Kalua ignored her, pulled in his hind legs, stretched out his front ones and calmly sat down facing the mat. When those on the mat began to eat, the goat too started chewing the cud. When the first piece of meat landed near Kalua, he thumped his tail twice in thanks. Politely, he kept sitting, stretched out his neck and picked up the meat. The meat tasted good. He chewed on it twice before swallowing it, licked his lips and nose clean, and waited. The second piece of meat flew. It landed between his front legs, right near his throat. He thumped his tail thrice in gratitude before he stood up. The piece of meat was softer and he swallowed it immediately. When the bone flew, it landed near the goat. Kalua moved towards it and the goat was startled. She had swallowed what she had just chewed and was waiting for fresh cud to rise from her throat into her mouth. No goat likes to be disturbed at such a moment. She put her hooves together, lowered her head, took aim with her horns and attacked. A bone was at stake, so Kalua, growling *humm humm*, pretended to counter-attack. Madam goat got scared and ran, forgetting that she was tethered, and fell with a jerk. Kalua could not have cared less. He picked up the bone and moved away. When he had gone as far as the rope would let him, he sat down to enjoy the bone. The long-haired gentleman got up and gave Kalua another good thrashing, this time with a rope.

For the next seven days Kalua stayed in the graveyard, surviving on half a stomachful of food and a generous amount of beatings. One night he thought of exercising his teeth on the rope that tied him.

After an hour of effort the surprising result was that Kalua found himself free.

The only sign of bondage remaining was the foot-long rope that still hung from his neck but Kalua did not care and set out. The thought of Chandu and a full meal gave his feet impetus. He crossed the shade of a neem tree and its roots; three graves covered just with earth, two solidly constructed ones and then another huge one next to that jujube tree, two sunken graves, one little grave next to a big one, one empty grave, and finally a broken section of the wall surrounding the graveyard—all this with his nose to the ground and his tail pointing to the sky.

A mongoose stood on the other side of the wall. Kalua saw him and leapt at it. The mongoose saw Kalua and ran. In four large bounds, Kalua caught up with it. The mongoose turned round, his tail now swollen into a bush, rose on his hind legs and prepared for battle. Kalua stopped—his front legs loose, his hind ones taut. Perhaps they apologized to each other because they went their separate ways. Kalua's nose went back to the ground and his tail to the sky as he renewed his search for the scent of either Chandu or food.

He soon reached the tarred road and walked on it until he reached the police post near Aish Bagh. A fat dog lying there growled *hoonn* without moving. Kalua's tail descended and he fled. He kept going till he smelt a bone. Then he stopped immediately, put his nose to the ground, sniffed *soonn soonn* a few times and found the bone. On examination, he found that a part of it could be of use to him. He dealt with it and moved on. When he reached the station of the Rohilkand–Kumaon railway line, an earless dog appeared and blocked his way. Standing arched, he showed all his teeth and drawing on all his patience, said *kheenss*.[4] Kalua

[4] In Urdu, *kheenss* means a grin which exposes the teeth.

too showed his teeth and answered *kheenss*. Missing-Ears said in a deeper voice, 'Let's see.' Kalua bared his teeth, jerked his head thrice, made faces and said *hain, hain, hain*. A bitch joined them. She smelt Kalua at both ends and then casually walked away which clearly meant, 'Let him be. He's a kid.' Bad-tempered Missing-Ears was not ready to give up, though. He pounced on Kalua with sounds of *huum, huum huum*. Helpless Kalua offered submission by lying down, utterly still.

For two months, as a subordinate of Missing-Ears, Kalua roamed the tracks of the Rohilkand–Kumaon railway from the Aish Bagh station to Agha Mir ki Deorhi. This was the territory that Missing-Ears had claimed with his teeth and his claws. Often, Kalua would walk farther in search of Chandu but he could not go too far because every inch of the city was divided into territories among the dogs and, according to their laws, stepping into another's territory was a crime. Even if he managed to cross the large territory of a single ferocious owner without being noticed, he would still have to face the owner of the next territory along with his protégées, and he was all alone. He did gain from these unsuccessful forays, though. The wounds strengthened him physically and he learnt the finer points of the art of war.

One day Kalua was returning from Agha Mir ki Deorhi. What did he see at a little distance from the railway crossing but the mangled corpse of his lord, Missing-Ears, on the railway track! The distressed mistress was standing there, sniffing him. What could Kalua do except offer condolences? He too went and sniffed and stood there with the mistress in her sorrow. He inherited the territory and took charge. The regular cuisine in this territory was the food that fell out of the trains and that which dropped from the claws of kites flying overhead. This was now shared between two instead of three. In just one month the mistress put on weight and her limbs became more agile. Falling in love made her feel young again and one day she left Kalua behind and followed a spotted dog. Kalua was left alone, the sole protector of the territory and the only claimant to its food. With a regular and generous supply of food and rigorous exercise, in a month Kalua was a different being—his coat a shiny, velvety black, his tail long and swaying, his muzzle stout and his muscles rippling. He was taller than the tallest dogs around. The vagrant, thieving dogs feared for their lives when he confronted them. He even extended his territory to include that half of the platform at Agha Mir ki Deorhi which had bordered his territory. One day, on this platform, he sensed a smell. His love-lorn heart missed a beat. Chandu had been sitting there.

Kalua smelt the spot, raised his head and stood still. If nature had given him tears, they would have flowed. For a long time he kept smelling the spot, nose to the ground and tail up in the air as usual. The scent of Chandu was distinct from the countless other smells around. Picking up her scent, he followed it. Alexander the Great could not have faced as many tribulations as Kalua had to deal with before he reached Bulochpur. He had to wound scores and was severely wounded himself. When he reached there, it was already one in the morning. It was the same lane, the same building and the same shop; but it was locked and everyone was asleep inside. He smelt the doors. The smell of both Chandu's parents was fresh but the scent of Chandu was faint. Dogs appeared, barked at him and moved on as Kalua sat in front of the shop and the scent of Chandu kept getting fainter. By four in the morning it had disappeared. He lifted his face and started wailing. If only some human had told him that Chandu had just gotten married and left with her husband for Bans Bareli. But who was there to do this? Instead, Chandu's father emerged with a staff in his hands saying, 'You won't stop crying will you, you cur?'

The dogs belonging to the butchers were neither as tough as he nor as well-built but they lived off raw meat and were ferocious. Kalua had a hard time until they finally left the lane and moved away to the open ground behind it. Kalua spent most of the day and night in front of the shop where no one recognized him any more. Chandu's parents constantly beat him but he would not leave the vicinity of their shop. Enough good food was available but unfortunately, the fire in his heart, the longing for a few drops of love, continued to blaze. After some time he flirted with others, begging for and offering love, but no one responded and another year passed. Eventually, one day, Chandu returned.

She was still the same although a bit thinner. She carried an infant in her arms but had completely forgotten Kalua. In fact, she was frightened of him. A human heart would have burst with happiness but Kalua was only a dog so all he could do was spread himself on the ground. He crawled on his stomach—his tongue stretched out—and moved forward to lick her feet. When they were not available, he licked the ground where they had been. When Chandu's slippers started hitting him, he lay down on the ground and closed his eyes. When her father's stick hit him, he crouched and whimpered. But nothing worked. In the mill of life, hearts are crushed instead of stones. Chandu returned to her husband's home on the eighth day.

The black dog today, a picture of rage and tyranny, roams around like a vagabond. Dogs are afraid of him and move out of his way when he approaches. His eyes are like two live red coals on his black face. The hairs on his thick neck stand straight and his tail stretches out stiffly.

The sweet little Munnan too has become a vagabond, thanks to the extreme temper of his father and his mother's unquestioning love. Instead of suffering constant scoldings and beatings at school, he had celebrated a day of freedom in the deserted *idgah*. It was four in the evening and he sat on the four-feet-high wall, wondering what he should do with the evening. Should he return home? They must have found out by now that he had not been at school and his little heart began to panic. Ever searching for love in the wilderness, Kalua passed that way. He saw the sad boy.

In the same way as night appears dark to humans while for dogs nights have a pleasant light, for humans the face is only a conglomeration of eyes, nose, ears and mouth but for dogs a face also includes the sparkle of happiness, the darkness of sorrow and the crimson glow of love. Kalua saw the sad boy sitting there but he kept walking, lost in his own world. He was walking alongside the wall and the scent of the boy was perceptible. Suddenly he felt something peculiar about it.

He had not been gifted with thought or memory for situations associated with thoughts. But he could not help himself. He turned round and looked at the boy.

Once, there had been an ocean of fire with waves of flames reaching for the sky. What happened when a baby in a basket was thrown into this inferno? In the twinkling of an eye, it turned into a verdant, flowering and wondrously scented garden in which a child was playing. This story is about the Prophet Ibrahim. Minds with an excess of intellect are unable to imagine this. Come this way, please.... Let me show them that the same thing can happen and perhaps even more wonderful things can happen. A buffalo cannot match a dog in violence. A grinding stone can be worn down but not a dog's constancy. When faced with the courage and ferocity of a dog, even a tiger backs off. Yet with one little sound of affection, the dog falls at your feet and becomes the living epitome of such complementary qualities as meekness, vulnerability and base abjection.

Munnan and Kalua began their friendship afresh. There was some buttery roasted bread left in Munnan's pocket which he crumbled and presented to Kalua. There was no more egg—not even the smell of it—yet, Kalua loved the bread. Hesitantly, Munnan stroked Kalua's head. Giddy with love, Kalua stretched himself out and uttered *aaonn*. Playing with the dog, making it run after stones he threw, Munnan headed home. He hoped that the news of his truancy from school had not reached home. Fearfully, he entered the house and Kalua stayed outside.

His doting mother washed his face, fed him and gave him an *anna* to get himself a kite. She also bought him iced candy for two *paise*. Twice she rose like a firm rampart between him and his father's fury. Munnan went to sleep as soon as night fell. What a pity, ignorant mother! You did everything but find out what was in his little heart. You can only access a child's heart by becoming a child yourself. In there are all his small sorrows, his tiny joys, his innocent grudges, but stupid mothers ignore these.

For six days Kalua sat resolutely outside Munnan's school and watched the goings-on. Finally, he could bear it no longer. The black creature, weighing thirty-five seers, entered and violently confronted the school teacher, knocked him down and mounted his chest. A weeping Munnan hurriedly collected his books and school bag and ran from the school. Once outside he called out *aaow aaow*, summoning Kalua, and began to run. Soon Kalua joined him, jerking his bloody ear. He lifted his head and tried to lick Munnan's face but Munnan hit him on the head with his writing slate. Kalua was delighted and romped off ahead of him.

The next day, his school bag under his arm, Munnan headed for the *idgah*. Kalua did not care where they went. When they reached the boundary wall of the waterworks they sat down under the overhanging branches of a tamarind tree. Munnan got out pilfered bread, meat and bones from his coat pockets and fed Kalua. Then, with a stone tied to a string, he tried to retrieve a kite tangled in the branches of the tamarind tree. Each time he threw the stone towards the kite, Kalua jumped even though he could jump only about a foot and a half high. After much stone-throwing, Munnan picked up a raw wood apple and headed towards Talkatora. Munnan ate the fruit, smacking his lips so loudly that Kalua began to drool but when he was given a piece he just sniffed at it and let it be.

The heavens overflowed with blessings
And in the drawing of lots, this fell to me!

Animals are given the gift of instinct in which there is no likelihood of mistakes while we who are given intellect—we stumble at every step.

On the third day, when Munnan returned home in the evening after a day of loafing, he spotted three schoolmates and a teacher outside his door. His father was at the door, talking to them. A shiver ran through him and he immediately turned back. He returned to the *idgah*. He roamed around there till it was dark and then his feet automatically headed for home. When he reached the waterworks, fear gripped his heart again. His mind made his feet stop. He climbed the boundary wall of the waterworks. It was completely deserted inside. A short way away were large tanks of stored water. He jumped from the wall and reached their edge. Kalua too jumped and was beside him. A wall, a foot and a half high, surrounded these reservoirs and in the clear water tiny fish swam. Munnan forgot his troubles and sat on his haunches, engrossed in watching them. A fish approached, Munnan bent over the wall to catch it and tumbled headlong into the water. Kalua was some distance away. He let out a small scream and jumped directly into the water. Before he could reach him, the boy was already headed towards the bottom. The water was very deep and it was quite a few minutes before the child arose again. Kalua's unfailing instincts told him the spot at which the boy would rise and he was waiting. He placed his body under the boy's chest like a shield. The boy had swallowed a lot of water and had nearly lost consciousness, yet he put one hand around Kalua's neck and with the other he gripped his hind legs.

The red of the sunset darkened into blackness. The stars which had been peeping out of the sky, finally shone brightly. A bat swooped across the surface of the water, took two drops of water in its mouth and rose again. Two hours later, a mongoose rose on his hind legs and looked at the water and then whizzed back into the bushes. The night continued to deepen. A star fell and disappeared into the Milky Way. Kalua's stomach had swollen and he had no strength left. He could keep either his nose above the water or the child's. The feelings in his heart were still as strong. The boy's nose stayed above the water and the dog's below. Some people gathered in the morning. They took the whimpering boy out of the water and ran towards the Medical College. They left Kalua's swollen corpse behind which was soon retrieved by two scavengers and thrown in the grounds outside the enclosure.

Three vultures swooped down from the sky. They pulled in their wings which spanned six feet and slowly started moving towards the corpse.

Biru

After the yogi's arrest, Biru became very irritable. Now that he was without the yogi's protection, the boys of the village started harassing him and Biru in turn started attacking any human he came across. The hostility between him and the villagers rapidly escalated until they began to pelt stones at him so that he was forced to leave not only the yogi's dwelling, but the village too. He looked back at the hut with a heavy heart, then crossed the railway tracks and walked to the abandoned brick kiln beside the canal. Here, he drove out the village buffaloes whose grazing place it was. Word spread in Khatima village that the yogi's violent nilgai[1] was now living in the brick kiln and people stopped venturing that way.

Biru liked the isolation at the kiln. He was not interested in humans and he scorned the beasts of the village. He believed that he and the yogi, who had raised him, had been born solely to love each other and that there was no other couple like them. For Biru, there was no other human like the long-haired, half-naked yogi nor was there another animal which could match his own majestic build, black coat, white collar, beautifully pointed beard and sharp horns. He felt lonely, but he distracted himself with memories of his time with the yogi. The yogi would sing songs and *bhajans* for him while he played his *iktara,* feed him gram

[1] Nilgai (*Boselaphus tragocamelus*) is commonly known as the blue bull though it is a part of the antelope family. (Editor)

soaked in salted water and scratch his neck. Then suddenly, the yogi was gone, Lord knows where, and Biru was miserable at the loss and his loneliness.

It was early winter and evening was settling in. Biru stood next to the pit he had chosen as his lair, stared at his reflection in the water, and occasionally lifted his head to look across the railway line at the village and the railway station of Khatima as it was swallowed up by darkness. Around him, he heard the musical chimes of bells as herds of cattle headed towards the village. Overhead, flocks of parakeets and crows called to each other as they headed out to spend the night in the forest. He grieved as he stared at himself in the water. The misery of being alone in this world overpowered him as he stood there. It was getting darker and there was melancholy all around. Behind him was the jungle, completely silent. Faint sounds came from the fading dwellings of Khatima.

Suddenly, he detected a slight movement behind him. He turned around to look and was taken aback. A nilgai, exactly like him, stood two yards outside the forest staring at him. The same white throat bib on its chest, the same black back, he was almost as high as Biru, but did not wear the necklace of cowries or the nose ring of a thin rope that was threaded through Biru's nostrils. Nor was his build as heavy as Biru's. However, Biru thought his lean, well-formed limbs very attractive. Biru's heart began to flutter as he slowly approached the visitor. The new nilgai too, wagging its flat tail, took a step towards him. As Biru drew closer to him, the desire to rub horns with his fellow being began to overcome him. The other nilgai also lowered its horns, jerked its head and came closer, but when they were just a few feet apart, the nilgai from the jungle noticed Biru's necklace and nose ring. He turned around immediately, darted into the forest and disappeared. Biru was surprised. He walked slowly towards the jungle and stared at its dark interior for a long time. He wanted to go in and find his fellow being but the jungle was dark and he was not used to roaming around in the dark. Helpless, he returned and found a high spot in the kiln, settled down comfortably and began chewing the cud, lost in thought. He frequently looked towards the jungle, hoping that his fellow being would reappear.

Very early the next morning Biru entered the jungle to begin his search. He walked far into the *sal* grove where little grass and few bushes grew under the tall trees. But as he proceeded, the *sal* trees got smaller and the jungle grew more dense. He began to find it difficult to walk amongst the undergrowth for he had always been used to walking in open, clean spaces. His limbs got entangled in the bushes and the creepers, but soon he began to enjoy this experience. He walked until noon and except for a few peacocks, he saw no animals. The jungle got thicker and more difficult to tackle so he turned back. When he emerged from the jungle, the day was ending. He entered the wheat field barricaded by thorny branches and began feeding on the green wheat. Wondering if the yogi had returned, he walked towards Khatima. On the way many villagers threw stones at him and he attacked them. When he got close to the yogi's hut he was welcomed by a stick-wielding, stone-pelting mob. Instead of finding the yogi, he found himself with many wounds. Helpless, he returned to the kiln. He could no longer dwell in the village nor did he want to stay at the kiln any longer. All he could think of was the jungle and what was in there for him? Biru turned bad tempered and depressed. Every evening he would stare at the spot where he had seen his look-alike.

One morning, Biru was walking away from the kiln alongside the forest where hundreds of thousands of massive tree trunks stood silently in the darkness created by their leaves. He heard a rustling among them and stopped. He looked intently into those thousands of pillars but saw nothing. He was about to move on when suddenly a number of animals moved and he saw them clearly. Among them was his look-alike, the black male nilgai and with him were four beautiful, lean and delicately-built cows at the sight of whom lightning seemed to strike Biru. A small herd of female fellow beings! He wished he could live with the females instead of the other male. In an instant it dawned on him that he had not been born only to keep the yogi company. His heart came alive. His despondency turned to hope, his sorrow to joy. He immediately trotted in, tearing through the thorny barricade between field and jungle without a thought.

A few of the females took a leap or two forward and then they all stood there, facing him. The owner of the herd, the wild male nilgai, stood in front, his horns ready to protect his harem. Either from instinct or because of the blood that ran through his veins, Biru knew that the victor in a fight between two males would be the owner of the herd and the vanquished would live by himself until he was able to defeat a male and take possession of his beautiful queens. Biru was not only proud of his strength but also desperate to acquire a herd. At this moment, he was even ready to fight an elephant if he had to and not accept defeat until he had shed the last drop of his blood.

Unfortunately, as soon as he neared his opponent, the females saw his necklace and got scared. Screaming *pi qoon, pi qoon*, they bolted. The male had no reason to stay on now for when the ladies themselves did not like the stranger, where was the need to fight? He followed his herd.

Biru was taken aback and stood still. Then he went in pursuit. His heavy frame was not used to running. The jungle became impenetrable and he could not see their hoof prints. However, he had caught their scent and began to follow it. This was a completely new experience for him. He had smelled thousands of different smells every day but had never paid any attention to them. Now he realized how important smell was. He walked for a long time and eventually emerged into a burnt out *chandar*. A strong wind blew and scattered all scents, leaving him helpless. There were no other animals in the clearing so he headed north, walking on the edge of the jungle. On the way he saw six female *chital*. They resembled the nilgais but in no way could they be compared to them in beauty. However, as soon as he got close to them they too scattered out of fear.

Until that day Biru had been indifferent to his own world, his fellow animals, his species and even his own being, for he had been living in the artificial world of humans where his status was no better than that of an unwelcome guest. The world of the humans could not involve him in any of its concerns nor could Biru take any part in any of its activities. The struggle to live involves every breath and this is what makes life interesting. It is the spring of the water of life. Biru had been living an uninvolved life, his stomach full of food that came to him unasked-for, heedless of joys and sorrows, unacquainted with desire or hope. He did not know of search and quest, love and hate; in fact, he was unfamiliar with any emotion. He had lived his life half-awake, his mind and senses dulled. He had done things which were of no consequence. Life had not kept him busy and he had not needed any diversions.

Suddenly, a real and pleasurable world had opened up for him. He could see his future life, clear and sharp. It was one for which he was born and where each leaf had been created to bring him countless pleasures. On entering the jungle, the senses he had been deprived of, were reborn. His ears began to twitch at the slightest of sounds; his nose quivered at smells from a few miles away; his shins began to deal with obstacles and find their own way; his sight began to pierce the darkness of the night. In a month Biru had turned into a wild nilgai. What a pity that the symbol of his slavery, the necklace of cowries was still around his neck. The rotting rope nose ring had got caught in a branch and snapped; the necklace, however, still made his life dismal. In the same way as the world of Khatima had driven him away because of his horns, the world of the jungle avoided him because of this necklace. At night he would see herds of *chital*, sambar, hog deer and nilgai grazing silently, side by side, in the *chandar*. However whenever he approached them, they all moved away. In the searing heat of the day when he would roam wildly in the grasses and bushes of the unburnt *chandar*, he often chanced upon animals sitting contentedly chewing cud. They would get up the moment they saw him, wag their tails, lower their heads and disappear in the narrow lanes of the grasslands. Unhappy and confused Biru had crossed many of the forest ranges—Khakhra, Lohiya, Soni Gurkha, Jagbura and had now reached the Chandni range of mountains, north-west of Mandi, bordering Nepal.

The Chandni ranges of mountains were a small part of a chain of mountains, the initial steps of the heaven-touching Himalayan range. It had neither the low temperatures of the mountains nor pine trees. The *sal* forest from the northern *Terai* continued to spread up the two thousand feet high peaks of the range, but this is where it ended. On the steep slopes to the north, among the large boulders and expanses of rock, grow evergreen bushes which first appear sparse but become denser down the slopes. In fact, they became so wild that they surrounded and hid the Kali River that flowed in the narrow valley between the Chandni range and the Gora Mountains of Nepal.

In embellishing this vegetation, nature had liberally used all its ornamentation. Plants grow like moss on the rocks. Each leaf among this dense foliage was a miracle of nature. Some felt like velvet and shone like silver; some were smooth and soft, delicate as silk; on some there was a red dot and on others, white stripes; some were sharp and could leave cuts. However, they were all green. Everywhere and all around green overlay green. There was green grass on the ground and over it, the bushes. Over these bushes spread creepers. There were flowers of all kinds with a variety of scents. Small bubbling springs of crystal clear water gently sang ragas all around as they avoided the rocks, gushed over boulders, wandered into the undergrowth on the slopes, as they descended to join the Kali river. The Kali flowed, rustling in little cascades, avoiding the large boulders gushing around the bends in the rocks, as it swayed on its ways through the middle of this garden.

Actually, this small valley is a part of the garden of paradise which is enclosed by the high Gora Mountains on one side and on the other by the steep precipices of the Chandni range. In this forest, in the cool shade of wild roses and cane grass, the king of the jungle, the eleven-feet-long, gold-coated, black-striped tiger, sleeps soundly during the day till the birds stop chirping and start huddling up for the night and hundreds of thousands of fireflies light up the river. The king then appears, yawning and muttering *aaown aaown* and strolls up to the river. The few *kankars* [2] who live there, bark as they flee up the slopes of Gora. There are few deer in this area for despite the abundance of trees, bushes and grasses, very little is edible. Food is far more abundantly available in the *Terai* and therefore the deer prefer to live on the slopes of Chandni.

[2] The *kankar* is a small deer which resembles a dog. Its coat is fawn like those of dogs and its teeth too resemble those of dogs. It also makes barking sounds. (Author)

However, when the two-legged creature enters the *Terai* with his thundering, fire-spewing sticks; the animals, terrified by these tyrants, climb the peaks of Chandni and descend the difficult and dangerous tracks and take refuge in the seclusion surrounding the Kali. Here they have to live in proximity of the tiger but they prefer this to being in the jungle where cruel and merciless humans have appeared. The tiger, even though he is a predator, lives in the jungle among his prey and is one of them, and they have learnt to live with him. He is their ruler to whom they have to offer the life of one of their herd every week as tax. But he is never cruel the way humans are. He never hunts unnecessarily or simply for the sake of killing and the fun of blood-letting. When his stomach is full, the animals do not even see him and if they do, he avoids them. He has no need to scare the other animals in the forest. When he is hungry, he is forced to pick on one weak member of a herd with such stealth and skill that when he grabs his victim, many within the herd do not even notice that one of them is missing. If the tiger's prey is large, he feeds on it twice or three times. Once he is satiated he disappears into a quiet, cool spot for four days from which he does not emerge except to quench his thirst. On the seventh or eighth day he needs to hunt again and emerges again at night, softly hiding in bushes and behind trees. He does not want to create fear or panic among the other animals. He believes himself the owner of the herds and amongst them he finds food in the same way as a wise gardener gradually picks vegetables from his fields. He hates ruining or wasting flesh. The animals are his crops and it is their offspring that keep his kingdom populated. When an animal grows old or weak and is no longer able to procreate, he picks on it quietly to feed himself as if it were a ripe fruit ready for plucking. The herds fear him but he does not grip their hearts with horror. When he hunts, it is like a game of *kabaddi* in which they are themselves equally involved. If one of them has to concede defeat to the tiger's swiftness and skills, the others have no idea what befell him subsequently. And then, what is it that befalls the prey? The tiger lands on it in a single jump which breaks its back instantly. In the next moment, the tiger jerks it twice which separates every vertebrae in its neck. In less than two minutes the victim is free from all pain. In complete contrast, when man, with death and destruction on his mind, barges into the forest, he upsets their world with fear and dread. He kills without reason and judgement, interested only in destruction. What is even more cruel is that he injures more animals than he kills and he leaves these animals soaked in blood behind, to die over days, weeks, even months, the most painful of deaths.

Sometimes the animals of Chandni too have to face the devastation caused by these wild men. But this is rare because between Tanakpur Mandi and these forests there are several dangerous swamps and dense jungles which protect the ranges. For years animals had been living here peacefully without fear or danger till suddenly one slight ripple disturbed their world. Biru had just arrived and like Majnu he began to follow the herds of nilgai. He would not let any herd stay in one place nor would he let the other animals chew their cud in peace. At first, the male head of the herd tried bravely and very hard to chase Biru away but when he faced a series of defeats at the hands of this demon-like opponent and also suffered a number of wounds, he stopped challenging Biru. From then on, whenever he spotted Biru from afar, he would fully posture for war, his horns pointed forward and his hooves firmly together but when his enemy came near, he would run. In the meantime, the females of his herd, having spotted Biru, would already have fled. The lean and fit wild nilgai would rejoin them in four giant leaps and the heavy-set Biru would once again start to pursue them in his slower gait.

The mountains of Chandni were still dealing with this problem when another calamity descended. A tall, irritable and bad-tempered white bear,[3] along with his wounded female, descended eight thousand feet from the snowy peaks across the Gora. After crossing Gora, the bears came to the banks of the Kali beyond which the female had no strength to proceed. A hunter's bullet had smashed her jaw and she could no longer eat. Beside the Kali, she lived off water. In pain from hunger and her wound, she began to wait in misery for death. During this while, the white bear, which is by nature bad tempered, became more so. Without discrimination he made life hell for all the animals, small or large. Whenever he came across an animal, he would growl *bhaaown bhaaown*, grab it and tear it apart. And then thrash the life out of it by dashing it to the ground. When he went and sat on the banks of the river, he cut off access to drinking water for the others. If he entered the *chandar*, he made it impossible for the herds in there to chew cud or sleep in peace. There was commotion everywhere. And when, on the eighth day, his injured female died, his temper became worse. Animals abandoned their grazing fields, changed their watering holes and their lounging areas were gone. The tiger too was very unhappy because of this disturbance. His prey had panicked and had become even more alert and he had to work very hard to feed himself. He would lie in wait along his regular tracks, behind rocks near watering spots or behind the thick trunks of the *sal* trees, yet no herds came by.

Today, he was again very agitated and angry. The fire of hunger had been raging in his stomach for two nights and now, when the third was beginning, he was desperate. He vigorously shrugged

[3] Himalayan brown bear.

his coat, licked his shoulders and legs clean and emerged from the dark recesses of a dense bush and headed towards the Kali, making sure that he stayed hidden in the bushes. An impudent rabbit behind him stopped and scratched himself and then disappeared. As soon as the tiger began to drink at the river, a peacock spotted him and shrieked. On hearing that, a dozen or so other peafowl in the area started to scream. Silence fell again. The tiger had his drink and then stared at the water for some time. He turned around and took a few steps before he stopped again. For a long time, he stood silently shaking his tail ever so slightly and moving his cupped ears around.

It was the eighth day of the moon and moonlight filtered through the leaves and fell on the tiger at a few spots. There was complete stillness; except for the soft sweet musical sounds of the water springs, there was silence. The beautiful, gentle, elegant and innocent tiger suddenly shivered. He had been trying to figure out something and he had just succeeded. Briskly he turned around again. In a trot he was quickly beside the Kali and then with his body still and with his limbs arched, he leapt across the river, casually. What was a distance of twelve feet for him? It did not take him long to gallop silently up to a pointed peak in the Gora, three hundred feet high. Here he sat down behind some rocks facing Chandni from where he could clearly see the jungles on both sides of the Kali and the sheer rise and the edges of the Chandni range. He had his tail by his side, his mouth was open, he panted slightly as he moved his eyes around and carefully watched the steep slopes in front of him. Suddenly he saw the bear, whose scent he had already picked up on the banks of the river, clumsily climbing up the slopes. His mouth closed, his tail fell behind him like a rod and its tip started waving like the head of a cobra. The tiger crouched. He was waiting for the bear to reach the top of the mountains and watching the route he was taking. The bear moved up slowly, using every stone, root or branch that he could find a foothold on till he finally reached the top under a huge *Aonla* tree where the ground was even, and then he disappeared beyond the edges. The king of the jungle then moved. Now, he indeed looked liked a tiger. He was by the river like lightning. Eight feet from the river, he leapt and flew in the air for thirty feet before he disappeared into dark bushes on the other side of the river to reappear two minutes later on rocks five hundred feet up, gliding up like a serpent. He was not going the way the bear had gone but was heading west of the tree to where the mountain rose straight as a wall. The tiger moved so fast up the climb that the eye could not keep pace. Then he was on a rock and before you knew it he was walking on a much larger boulder. Eventually, he reached a spot where not only was the mountain as straight as a wall but twenty feet above, a rock jutted out like a canopy. He stopped, gathered all four of his paws, bent down till his chest and stomach touched the rock and before you knew it he had leapt onto a ledge. At this point, there were no rocks or boulders jutting out. Now, at the final leg, there was only the thousand feet high wall-like mountain and on the top, a boulder sticking out between two large rocks. The tiger now took a very narrow and dangerous path which after many turns and winding like a serpent, eventually reached the boulder.

Man or beast, when possessed by love, becomes indifferent to pain and hardship and in this madness is ready to face any suffering, even the wilderness of the desert of Nejd. The sides of mountains burst and springs of milk begin to flow from them, the jewels in thrones and crowns fade in brilliance before a dim flame in a dark hut and all boasts wane at the cry of the heart. And since passion is a wild emotion (as every human over forty-five must know, whether he acknowledges it or not), Biru was particularly affected by it. The airs of the fidgety females, their sweet calls and their smells more intoxicating than musk or ambergris, created havoc in his frantic heart. The wild male nilgai, tired of the relentless pursuit and the constant moving, weakened by hunger and thirst, crippled by wounds, was beginning to get weaker by the day. Finally, early one evening when the bright light of the day was fading, the pleasant darkness of the night was descending, the ever present dew had begun to drip from the tall trees and two wild birds, two miles apart, were arguing, *tara tu tu tu*, the wild nilgai ran away for the last time from challenging Biru and accepted abject defeat. He rid himself of his passive defence, abandoned his females and ran away in the opposite direction from Biru. The abandoned herd, without its male protector, stood watching from the slopes, a hundred and fifty feet high. Biru moved in their direction but as usual, the females ran away from him. Biru did not know what to do except, perhaps, chase the wild male again and inflict obvious humiliation on him, perhaps even kill him. The wild nilgai, on the other hand, had left his problems behind and headed for the top of the Chandni mountains from where he intended to walk east and find his way down to the thick forests of khair (*Acacia catecu*). When he reached the two large rocks between which the huge boulder jutted out, at the height of a thousand feet, the tiger was already there. The tiger had come there to teach the bear a lesson but he sorely needed food for he was very hungry. He saw the old, wounded nilgai walking close by. Between the two rocks, which were nearly twelve to fourteen feet thick, there was a three feet wide passage. The tiger jumped and felled the nilgai. He jerked it a few times and his prey was still. According to habit the tiger wanted to drag it to a concealed, isolated spot before he began to feed but his stomach was aflame from hunger. However, since there was a large rock behind him and the boulder was a lonely place, he thought it reasonable to have a small snack there itself. From his neck, which had been pierced by thorns, there was a steady flow of blood, so he first licked this blood clean. Then, he slowly sank his teeth into the rump of the nilgai. With his paws he gripped its thigh and waist and then jerked his head. There was a sound of snapping. A piece of nilgai flesh, weighing a seer and a half, left the leg and was in the tiger's mouth. The bear, which happened to be passing behind the rocks, stopped when he heard this snapping sound. He moved his large furry head around and smelt the air—there were two scents mixed together. Angered, he cleaned his nose with his paw twice and then headed straight for the space between the two rocks. The tiger reacted with lightning speed. He left his kill, stood up and turned around. The bear shrugged a storm with his coat and rose on his hind legs, seven feet high and three feet wide like a furry monster, and blocked the way. The bear knew he had made a mistake, the situation was grim and he could not retreat now. If he was to move even an inch, the tiger would grab him. So he stood straight, his front paws stretched in front of him, ready for battle. A tiger always avoids a face-to-face confrontation. Now he was confronted by this demon that was waiting for him. How and from which angle could he attack he wondered! The two opponents stood facing each other thus for a minute. The tiger was hoping the bear would bend even a little so that he could attack his back. The bear was hoping for the crouching tiger to rise so that he could get under his stomach. With these tactics in mind the bear bent slightly and the tiger sprang. The claws of the tiger's front paws embedded themselves in the bear's rib and his fangs held his spine near his waist. The bear's large head and his front paws, with their long pointed claws were under the tiger's stomach. In a moment, the tiger's intestines spilled out entangled in the bear's claws.

While this was happening Biru was as usual wandering, haunted and blinded by the ghosts of passion. He was following the scent of the wild nilgai, indifferent to all other smells. Soon he had reached the spot where the wild nilgai was. As soon as he had walked in between the rocks, he saw the spectacle. On the jutting out bolder the nilgai lay lifeless to one side. On the other side, two mighty beasts were wrapped in battle. Biru too was proud of his strength and nature had taught him to attack when in danger. His head lowered itself and his neck tensed till it was like a tree trunk. The beast weighing nine maunds was ready to throw all his weight in the charge. He took too steps backward and when he leapt forward and butted them, the tiger and the bear, rolled over three times and then shot over the boulder and fell a thousand feet below.

On the boulder stained by their blood, lay Biru's necklace which he looked at sadly. The tiger had hit out at him with his paw but missed, broken his necklace but had not hurt his neck. When the tiger and bear, having covered the thousand feet of air, landed on another boulder, there was a thunderous thud which kept echoing in the valley. The echo had not died down when there was another crash with the sound of which the hills around the valley echoed again. Biru had pushed the corpse of the nilgai too off the ledge. The blood stained boulder was empty now. There was silence all around. Biru stood there silently. Then he heard the sweet sounds of *pi qoon, pi qoon*. To the west of him, on a peak a hundred feet from him stood the females watching, and calling out to him.

He went and joined them.

Gori ho Gori[1]

It was a monsoon night. A wet, cool breeze was blowing. The crickets were making a racket. The frogs were croaking *tar, tar, tar*. Sitting on the thick, dried branch of pipal, an owl called *huk hu, huk hu*.

Basanti turned on her side. Then she slapped her face and said, '*Hai re*! *Arre* Ram, look at these mosquitoes.' On the pipal tree the owl cried, *huk hu, huk hu*.

A six-month old child lay next to her. Basanti put her arm across it and muttered, 'He's back again, and the noise he makes! May he be destroyed.'

Huk hu, huk hu.

'*Aji o ji! Aji! O ji*. Get up. The owl is hooting and it is scaring me.'

Madho jerked her hand away, irritated. 'Let me sleep. It is not going to devour you.'

'Get up, come on, get up. I am frightened. Will you chase it away?'

'Your fears can go to hell,' Madho grumbled as he got up, rubbing his eyes. He lowered his legs from the cot and then immediately pulled them back up. Worried, he looked down, and then, all around him. It was a small mud house. In the dim light of a lantern blackened by its own broken chimney, he saw the courtyard shimmering. There was water all over the house.

[1] All the dialogue in the story are in Awadhi.

'What is going on?' Madho exclaimed.

Basanti sat up with a start. 'What are you looking at?' she said. '*Hey* Ram, wake up Bhiku. *Arey*, wake up Ramkalia. Get the bed, water has come. *Arey* Bhiku, Ramkalia! Ho, *arey* Ramkalia, you continue to sleep. *Arey* get up. And you Bhiku.'

The thin eight-year-old Ramkalia woke up. So did the six-year-old Bhiku. The not-yet-weaned infant woke up and began to cry. The other two cried too. 'O dear mother. O dear father, help us. O dear mother.'

'Be quiet,' Madho scolded. He tried to listen to the sounds in the silence. Basanti too paid attention to them. From somewhere far away there were sounds of *gharrup, shal shal shal, gharrup, shal shal shal*.

Huku hu, the owl called out.

Basanti weeping, shrieked out aloud, 'O brother Preetam, the flood is here. O lord what will become of my children?'

The children jumped from their small cot, splashed through the water and clung to their mother. Madho got up and went towards the door to check. Basanti screamed, '*Aji* where are you going *ji*?'

Someone called out from outside. 'Brother Madho *ho*. O Madho. *Arey*, it is a flood. Get up *re*, get up.'

Shurrup, ghurrup, shar shar shar. The sounds of flowing water were increasing alarmingly.

Mumm mumm, hain,[2] the goat said. Elsewhere, the cow called *maan, haan aan, maan haan aan*. In the twelve households of Gujarpurwa, there was panic. Everyone was up. All began to run. Some called out, some cried out and others wept.

Madho placed Ramkalia on the steps and with Bhiku in his arms, he began picking up a few things. Basanti, with her infant daughter

[2] Sounds like: 'There is water here.'

in her lap, picked up the bunch of corn cobs, caught hold of one of the floating pots and with her leg stopped the urn which was trying to drift past her. The bed shook its head and then it too turned. The *durrie*, the sheet and coverlet were all on it. There, it too floated!

Outside the house, men and animals were screaming. Inside the house, Ramkalia and Bhiku were crying. The sounds of water were the same both inside and outside the house. Basanti and Madho were still after their belongings. There was a roar, 'Run, run. O Basanti come out. *Arre* Madho run!'

The water shook. It jumped from the calves and reached the thighs.

Voices from outside called out, 'Run, run, brother Madho run. *Arey*, what is going on? Why are you not coming out?' The water shook again, moved back and then forth as it came up to their waists.

Basanti pleaded, 'O my anklets, o my necklace, get them.'

'Go, go, you get out and I will follow. *Arey* at least let me take some flour and salt and grab some bedding.'

The water roared. Four men were shouting. There were assaults on the door which gave way. The men came in. They caught hold of Madho and Basanti and began to pull them. 'Leave everything and come. Just save your lives. Come, come on.'

In the confusion, alarm, darkness, crying out for her clothes, her grain, the storage bins, trembling for her utensils and jewellery, Basanti implored: 'O brothers! Will someone take Ramkalia.' The lantern had gone off by now. In the dark, a voice replied, 'I will pick her up. You, you go. Go on, get out.'

The sounds of the lapping water, the dark night, the thunder and the lightning; with water up to their waists or chests, twenty to thirty humans and fifty to sixty animals were on the move. Every human was speaking. Every animal was calling. If one fell, another would pick him up. One would sink and another would pull him up. They left the village and at first walked together as a group and with care. They went through the mango grove towards the raised railway track three-quarters of a mile ahead. As they moved in the darkness, they began to get separated from each other.

Madho and Basanti were holding each other's hands. The infant and Bhiku was with them. They were confident that someone had also picked up Ramkalia from the stairs but Madho was worried about his cow and four bullocks which were with his brother-in-law who lived in a small hut near the well outside the village. Basanti was not so concerned about the animals. She was now fretting for her brother, 'He lives all alone out there. Who knows if he even woke up? Did he leave or not?' Supporting his wife who had stumbled, Madho repeated, 'Who knows whether he woke up or if he untied the animals or not.'

The night was so dark that one hand could not find the other. The water was above their waists. The people continued to separate. There was noise all around, some from near and some from far.

'Janaki, O Janaki!'

'I am here, brother.'

'Murli! *re* Murli!'

'I am fine. Keep moving.'

Madho was continuously calling out to his brother-in-law, 'Naga O Naga.' But there was no reply. The water flowed more forcefully and loudly. Someone called out, 'There is a drain alongside the track.' Another called out, 'Keep moving, carefully.' Another shouted, 'Brothers, do not give up, keep moving, the track is almost here.'

From the dark came Naga's voice, 'O brother Madho. Has anyone seen brother Madho?'

Someone answered, 'How are we supposed to have seen him? We cannot even see our hands.'

Madho quickly answered, 'All is well. I am coming. Did you bring the animals?'

'Where is Basanti? I do not hear her?' Naga called back.

'She is with me. Where are the animals? Did you bring them?'

'Come on, come on,' Naga shouted. They were at the tracks of the Rohilkand Kumaon rail line and Naga stood on it, two yards above the water.

The belching buffaloes, screaming cows, whining goats, crying children, frightened women, yelling men, all dripping wet, climbed on to the railway track. In the lonely night, the deserted track suddenly came alive. At the top of their voices people started enquiring about who was there and who had not. Everyone was worried about someone. They took a census of the population of the small hamlet. Both humans and animals were counted. The animals were all there. Among the males, the son of a *Chamar* and two *Kurmi* brothers were not there. Among the children, Ramkalia was missing.

Basanti and the *Chamaran* began to weep inconsolably for their children. The relatives of the two *Kurmi* brothers were not worried because both the brothers were good swimmers. They had also been asleep on a very sturdy and high platform in their maize field, which was on high ground.

Ramkalia's mother was weeping convulsively. Everyone was consoling her and trying to give her hope. 'Do not cry, be strong. Perhaps one of the *Kurmis* have reached her and taken her up a tree with him. There was also the *Chamar*'s son. Was he not the one who had agreed to carry her? He might have taken her and climbed a tree.' But how could a bereft mother stay quiet? Her heart was breaking. Madho was standing and weeping. Naga was sobbing convulsively and Gori the cow was there too uttering prolonged, loud moans. *Too kaan aan eh, too kaan aan eh.*[3] She too was a grief-stricken mother. The others might not have noticed, but she too had lost her calf. And when she cried, all she could utter was *too kaan aan eh*.

The cow walked up to the weeping Basanti. Basanti threw her arms around her neck and began wailing.

'O Gori (Gori *re*), my Ramkalia…*eeeh eeeh eeeh eeeh*….

O Gori, who will now take you out to graze…*eeeh eeeh eeeh eeeh*….

O Gori, who is going to feed you…*oooh oooh oooh oooh*….

O Gori, your Ramkalia…*eeeh eeeh eeeh eeeh*….'

The cow let out the same long moan *too kaan aan eh*.

Whether people know it or not but Ram knows what is in one's heart. The cow moaned and Basanti sobbed the night out. In the first light of day, everyone's eyes turned towards Gujarpurwa. There was a small mango orchard in front and this hid a part of Gujarpurwa. There was nothing left. The mango trees were there but the houses had been swept away. If any of the mud houses had survived, they would be the ones hidden by the trees for all one could see was the grove whose trees, their green arms spread wide were swaying in the water. Beyond them, as far as the eye could see, lay miles and miles of water. Water was flowing swiftly in the small drain next to the railway track. Yet four young men found the courage, tightened their loin cloths, and jumped into the water. They swam to the mango grove. There they found the *Kurmi* brothers and the son of the *Chamar* but not Ramkalia. The *Chamar* did not know how to swim and he was also very scared. They found

[3] Sounds like: 'Where are you?'

a plank which had got caught in the branches of a tree and was swaying in the water. They tried to talk the *Chamar* into holding the plank so that they could then steer him to safety. The boy refused to comprehend this for he was dying of fear. He just would not get into the water. They reasoned with him, pleaded with him but he did not agree. When they would move away leaving him behind in the tree he would yell and cry. One of the men finally thought of a solution. He climbed the tree the *Chamar* was on, caught hold of him by the neck and when he hit him hard a few times, the *Chamar* agreed. Holding the plank, he floated between them and the rest took turns at pushing the plank forward. On the way, one of them said, 'Now tell us truthfully or we will drown you right here.' The poor guy told all. Yes, he was frightened and was with the four men who had gone to get Madho and his family out and when Basanti had shouted he had said that he would carry Ramkalia. All the others had left in a hurry and when he was left alone, he too ran away. Once outside, he did not find the others and the water had risen further. When he reached the mango grove, he no longer had the courage to continue walking alone. So he climbed a tree. On hearing this, all of them said, 'Let us drown this sinner. What is the point of saving someone so wicked?'

However, they did not drown him but took him to the railway track.

There they found eager Relief Committee volunteers, somewhat more important and slightly arrogant Congress leaders given to little work but a lot of talk and police constables in red turbans strutting about arrogantly. Each was trying to help in his own way. Oil, *ghee*, flour, wood, lentils—all had been brought by the members of the Relief Committee. Safety arrangements were made by the police. The Congress leaders had brought small tents and medicine for first aid. In a little while everyone was happily preparing a meal. The *karahis* were set on the fire and *puris* began to be fried in these woks. Those who had hurt themselves while walking in the water in the dark were given first aid. But who could dress Basanti's wounds? Madho and Naga too were upset. Gori had been the only co-sufferer and she too was no longer there. Who knows where she went at day break?

While it was dark, the sounds of the water had frightened the yard-high Ramkalia no end and she passed the night crying till she was almost lifeless. When the faint light of day appeared, she was horrified. At one glance she noticed that there were no houses and no village left. More than half of the roof of her house had been swept away. She found herself sitting in a corner and in the other corner was a coiled snake, hissing and showing its forked tongue. All around her was water from which a few trees peeked out here and there. Behind her was the half drowned mango grove, from which emanated all kinds of waves. In fear and dread she screamed and screamed again. Terrified, she looked around. Let alone a human, she saw no living being—just her and the black cobra. And there was water and more water in which tiny whirlpools appeared and then disappeared with the sounds of *hurrup, hurrup*.

She covered her eyes with her hands and was muttering, 'O mother dear, O my mother!' when she heard the cow. '*Too kaan aan eh.*'

Ramkalia was startled. She removed her hands from her eyes. On her lifeless face covered with tears, a small smile appeared.

'*Too kaan aan eh,*' the sound came again.

'*Hare* Ram, it is Gori!' she said and looked all around. She could not see the cow but with all her strength she shouted, 'Gori, *ho* Gori!'

'Too kaan aan eh,' came the reply.

Then the swimming cow emerged from the grove. Ramkalia called out again. The cow, still calling, started to come towards her but then another sound came from far away. *'Oo maan aan eh.'* [4]It was the sound of her calf from behind the grove. The cow turned towards this call. Ramkalia's tiny heart began to sink. She was exhausted from crying all night, yet she summoned all her strength and called out, 'Gori, *ho* Gori.'

'Gori *ho* Gori!'

'O Gori dear, come here.'

'O dear mother, she is not coming.'

'Gori, *ho* Gori.'

'O Gori mother, please come.'

Gori did not change directions but she did turn her head around a few times and looked towards Ramkalia. She called out in anguish but she continued to swim towards the spot from which the calf was calling.

As soon as she crossed the grove she saw her calf floating at the same spot where she, her calf and the bullocks had been tied the evening before. Now, there were no fields, nor was there a hut. All that was there was water. The cow kept responding to her calf's calls till she reached it. She swam around it and smelt it. Once she even licked its mouth and then she began to swim away but the calf did not follow, staying afloat where he was. The cow returned, swam around it, gave it a push with her waist and stomach and then swam away. When the calf did not come, she returned again. She now understood what the problem was. He was tied to a peg stuck in the ground six feet below and the rope was just long enough for the calf to keep its nose above the water until then. If the water were to rise even by an inch, the nose too would be

[4] Sounds like: 'O Mother, I am here.'

covered. Despondent, the cow left her screaming calf there and once again headed towards Ramkalia.

Ramkalia, exhausted from weeping and screaming, had till now bravely battled fear, dread and eventually disappointment; she was, after all, only a little child of eight. When the cow reached her, she lay in a faint on the edge of the collapsing roof. Gori called out a few times and when Ramkalia did not respond, she licked her face with her long, rough and warm tongue. The girl regained consciousness. She was scared at first then she saw Gori. Saying, 'Gori mother, Gori mother!' she clung to her neck. Gori took two strokes with her legs and began to move. Ramkalia was pulled off from the roof and into the water. She thrashed her legs around in fear, clung to Gori and finally climbed on to her back. There she clung to her and lay flat like a lizard. Gori went to the calf again and tried what she had done earlier. She encircled it a few times and then swam away again. When the calf again did not follow her, she swam back to it again. Ramkalia now understood what the matter was. As soon as the cow reached the calf again, still lying flat on the cow's back, she extended a hand and undid the knot around the calf's neck. The calf was free. Both the cow and the calf began to swim. Ramkalia was clinging to the cow. The water was flowing away from the grove and the railway track so these two swam against the flow and after two and a half hours of circuitous swimming they climbed up the railway track. The spot they had reached was three miles away from where the villagers were. They had been at it from very early in the morning and when the brave village swimmers had reached the grove there had been no signs of the calf or Ramkalia. When the swimmers had reached Madho's house, the remaining part had been swept away too. At noon, when Gori with Ramkalia riding her, the calf following her and conversing in phrases of *Oo maan aah eh,* reached the villagers, there was commotion. They jumped with delight. Basanti, in her joy, was howling as she cried. Sometimes she hugged Ramkalia and sometimes the calf. She would cling to Gori who would say, '*Too maan aan eh, Hum maan aan eh.*'[5]

A voice called out, 'Say Gori *ma ki jai.*'

Fifty voices hailed her.

Again, the voice called out, 'Say, *jai* mother cow!'

[5] Sounds like: 'You are a mother, I am a mother.'

The Mirror of Wonders

When days start extending their life by casually bullying the nights, the dispirited nights find it hard to disperse the heat that has rained on them all day. The night runs out before the inflamed earth has time to cool. Another bright day peeps over the eastern horizon, and the humiliated darkness shrinks from the hills, rivers, fields and cities and goes to hide in the west. This happens day after day. The nights cannot cool the earth before the day appears, raining even more fire and turning the world into a hot oven.

The fields are ablaze, flames rise from the earth, buildings and homes become suffocating, roads are deserted, the air is full of dust and the *loo* blows relentlessly. Embers rain down.

Even during this period, when fields are drying up, plants burning up and trees withering, there is a part of mother India that is still peaceful and quiet.

Leaving the dead, dry, dusty, scorching, glowing, shining fields, weakened and thirsty birds fly miles and miles, and keep flying north till, surrounded by dense green forests, the dark, sacred gold and silver Himalayas, sparkling brighter than diamonds, appear, wearing a crown of snow. The tired, thirsty, melancholic flocks of birds immediately start chirping. They put all their energies into covering this last lap towards their goal and disappear into the wide green folds of the mountains.

This is another world. The air is cool, the ground is cool and so are the rocks. Between the rocks flow small cool springs. Cold, clear water from the snow drips at one place and elsewhere it sparkles and gurgles in tiny streams as it flows, sometimes skirting rocks, sometimes jumping off them onto slabs and then from slabs on to the rocks, it runs and gurgles into springs, humming, smiling and laughing. On all sides are small and large trees and under these trees are bushes and plants. Under these is velvety grass and moss. Bulbuls and Shamas sing ragas. Life is nourished in every way. Flowers smile everywhere. Everything is lush. Everything is fresh. Even the dust on the ground is green. The rocks are covered with green moss. The trees' branches and leaves are green. Large branches are alive with ferns growing on them, as if they want their own gardens, independent of the other branches.

Who does not crave for this life giving, soul uplifting climate? Only those ordained by Allah—be they animals, birds or humans—are lucky enough to be here.

It is the scorching month of June. The blazing earth is a stone slab, the sky shining like burnished copper. Gusts of hot wind slap everything. The sun is glaring, glowing, blinding and burning. Three beings are travelling towards the still far, faint, dark, mountains. One is human, the second an animal and the third—well, the third cannot be counted as a human and is not an animal. The third is a hill porter who, in search of work and tempted by wages, blundered down into this flat, boiling inferno three days ago and is now tumbling and struggling on his way home. He is drenched in sweat, struggling to breathe and is dizzy. He is at the crossroads of life and death. He will be lucky if he reaches home alive. He is walking slowly on the glaring, lonely road of Kathgodam where whirlwinds blow, his restrained hill-walk making him look like a clown. A woollen cap which covered his ears hangs from a string around his neck onto his chest. He has placed a folded blanket on his head, which forms another layer over his thick, shaggy hair. On his back is a basket made of bamboo. He is wrapped in a filthy cloak—which is an assortment of all kinds of woollen scraps and rags, patched in places with leather and fur, completely soaked in sweat. On his legs he wears a *pajama* made of thick cloth, widely flared, but narrow at the ankles and free of any unnecessary gusset. Below the *pajama*, his feet are encased in shoe-like cases made of sackcloth, coarse broad tape and canvas. Bent forward, he thuds along, climbing this even road. The slit, red, gum-filled eyes on his mongoloid face look longingly towards the mountains rising in the north and then they race over the endless straight road ahead and get absorbed in the dust of space.

Because of the heat, the thirst, the *loo* and the sunlight, the trees sometimes start to jump and dance; the straight road twists and sways. Sometimes, the brightness of the sun increases till it turns black and the world becomes dark. At times he stops his unsteady feet, bends down, puts his hands on his knees and waits. Darkness gradually descends. Then in the blinding, scorching sunlight, the leafless trees on both sides of the road start playing with each other. The road starts wriggling like a snake and he hears a sound, *ghain ghain*. Are the trees making this sound or the road? The trees are running, fading and then disappearing. Then there is darkness.

Ghain ghain, shaan, Khaj. A yellow Buick car stopped three feet from him. 'I am in trouble and that man is dead,' the driver said to himself.

Sounds of *Shain shain, chhan chhan, chhan chhan, shain shain, chhan chhan* emerged from the car's radiator.

'Move it, move it, hurry up,' ordered Ishtiaq Ali Sahib Qureishi, the aristocrat from Badayun.

The driver opened the door and jumped out swiftly. He went to the hill dweller, pushed him to the side of the road and came back.

Wavering, trying to steady himself, the hill dweller rose and approached the car, muttering something in his language. 'What is it?' Qureishi asked him rudely.

The driver stopped the car that had been crawling. He thought that Qureishi was telling him to stop. The hill dweller presumed Qureishi was calling him and drew nearer.

Qureishi Sahib asked, 'You! What is the matter?'

Breathing heavily, the hill dweller gasped, 'Water! Water, sir.'

Qureishi Sahib looked at the thermos flask and the earthen goblet covered with cooling *khass* and said, 'Ahmad give him some water from the tin can.'

'If there was any water in the can, I would have put it into the radiator—look, it's steaming.' The driver shook the can with his foot and said, 'There is some, enough for him to drink.'

Ahmad opened the petrol can and then, still sitting in the car, extended it out of the window and tilted it, 'Hey, here's the water.' He muttered to himself, 'The water is boiling. He can enjoy his tea.'

The hot water worked like an elixir on the hill-dweller. His eyes opened. The water ran out but his hand stayed cupped to his mouth and when he realized there was no more, he wiped his face with his wet hand, looked at Qureishi Sahib and said, 'You are going to my land. I'm going there too. Can I go with you, Sahib?'

'You want to come with me, you pleasure seeker?' Qureishi Sahib said. 'You want to sit on this?' he asked, pointing to the seat of the car.

The hill-dweller tried to get in to the back seat where Qureishi Sahib was sitting, by raising a leg and putting it through the window. Alarmed, Qureishi Sahib moved back. '*Arey, arey*, how dare you, you ape! I give an inch and you take a yard. Do you want to sit in my lap? Get away, go there. Ahmad, open the door and let him sit in front with you.' The car began to move again.

Far ahead, by the side of the road, sitting on the masonry around a well, was the third traveller. True, the female monkey was a beast but monkeys are the first link in man's evolution. A lizard-like baby, not more than three or four days old, nothing more than a lump of flesh, clung lifelessly to her. The monkey was sitting on the rim of the well and peering into it. Her face showed that she was under extreme pressure and depressed. The clear cold water in the well smilingly held out another strange image—there is the circle of another well and another monkey with a baby peeping into it. The monkey's paw dislodges a tiny piece of the crumbling masonry which drops into the well. The surface of the water breaks into smiles. The strange image is disturbed. The need for water overcomes the monkey but the water is out of reach. She vigorously scratches her head twice, perches on the edge of the well and looks around.

Below the rim of the well is a small patch of damp earth. The monkey jumps up and goes and sits on it. She touches the wet earth with the palm of her hand. With her nails, she scratches and lifts about a *tola* of it in her hand but immediately throws it away. Instead, she picks up an old match box lying there, tears it apart and throws it away, and then goes back to the rim of the well and peeps inside. There is water and also a reflection in the water! Surprised, her eyebrows rise and then shrink, indicating deep thought and deliberation. But these are all external signs. Wonder and astonishment, pain and suffering, love and jealousy, affection and envy, need and quest produce evil fruit. The mind is devoid of reflection which comes from continuous thought. Emotions are superficial. Compassion is subservient to brutality.

Shaan, the car arrived and stopped with a crunch. The water in its radiator was boiling...*sheen sheen, sheen sheen, chhun chhun, chhun chhun chhun*. The monkey took two leaps onto the tree close by and then, in one move, she jumped to its top branch. From there, for some time she chattered at the car; when no one paid any attention to her, she turned away from the well and sat there, uninterested in the humans, with a tranquil, serious and indifferent look on her face.

'Get up, come on, get up,' Ahmad urged the hill-dweller after he had himself jumped out of the car and tried to push the hill-dweller out as he extracted a thin rope from under his seat. He tied it to the can, walked to the well, drew water from it and started to pour it into the radiator. When the hill-dweller saw this, he impatiently gathered himself, untangling his rags from the steering, gears and levers, squeezed himself out of the car and sat next to Ahmad with his hand cupped to his mouth. 'Some water, friend. Friend, water.'

The friend, Ahmad, casually continued to pour water into the radiator. The can emptied, and he went back to the well to fill it again. The hill-dweller went with him and sat below the ledge of the well with his hand cupped to his mouth. 'Sir, water. Water, sir.' Ahmad filled the can and when he moved towards the car, leaving the hill-dweller next to the well, Qureishi Sahib called out from the car, '*Arey*, let him have some. Give him a drink first.' The arrogant driver paid no attention and again began to pour water into the radiator. The hill-dweller got up and came close to Ahmad. The can was still a little more than half full when the radiator overflowed. Ahmad signalled to the hill-dweller to sit down. He sat, with his hand cupped to his mouth, and drank till the can was empty. 'The bastard will not stop drinking,' Ahmad said. The bastard asked for more water. Ahmad filled the can for the third time and poured out more water. When the hill-dweller had had his fill, Ahmad poured the remaining water next to the well and the two returned to the car. The car buzzed and then began humming and raking up the dust covered road.

As soon as the car moved the monkey jumped from the tree and came to the spot where the water had been poured. Most of it had by now been absorbed by the parched earth. A little more than a cup remained in a palm-sized depression. She put her front limbs on the ground, and bent down over it. She drank a little and then, with her hands still resting on the ground, she straightened up, bent her head to look at her baby, and then bent down to the water again. When there was no more water left, she got up in the same way. With one hand she pulled at the wet fur on her chin, then bent down and straightened up again. There was no more water. She put her palm on the slush and then licked it. She did this a few times and then with one hand patted the baby clinging to her chest. Then, raising her tail, she began to walk along the road in the shade of the trees.

In the meantime, the heated, humming car, fighting the gusts of *loo*, raising dust and getting coated with more dust, growling *ghain ghain* at passersby, swallowing miles, was now far away. On both sides of the road, numerous stone boundaries and a few houses indicated their proximity to Kathgodam. The slopes of the hills which earlier had been faintly dark now began to appear coated in green trees. They passed a few bullock carts and occasionally, gloomy wayfarers. Soon courtyards, with their low boundary walls and their banana and papaya trees hiding the houses behind, began to appear in quick succession. The car entered the city and passed through the market. Here, the car saw many of its fellow beings, predominant among which were members of the lorry tribe. Our car passed many petrol stations, ignored them, and finally came to a stop at the last petrol pump of the city. This was the last stop on the north of the city and beyond it, the climb up the hills began in earnest. Ahmad stopped the car, got out, wiped the dust off his face with a handkerchief and then pushed the hill-dweller, who was now suffering from a heat stroke, out of the car. His body was burning and his chest was on fire. The poor fellow misunderstood and sat down again, his hand cupped to his mouth.

'Ah you lucky loafer, got a free ride, did you not?' Ahmad said softly as he began to take stock of the petrol in the car. The petrol pump attendant arrived. After putting four gallons of petrol into the car they began to carefully drain the thick rubber hose of all the petrol. The petrol pump attendant scrutinized the hill-dweller and softly asked Ahmad, 'Where did you find this one?'

'He forced himself on us,' Ahmad said. 'Sahib let him ride with us. If you have water, will you get him some? The oaf is dying.' Ahmad then approached Qureishi Sahib and asked, 'Is there anything I can do?' The Sahib gestured. Ahmad carefully poured out water from the earthen goblet, added ice from the thermos and gave it to Sahib and then, hiding behind the car, had a drink himself. He placed the *surahi* and the thermos back in their places, and moving pieces of ice in his mouth from cheek to cheek, he went back to his seat. Water had arrived for the hill-dweller too. When he returned after his drink Ahmad asked him, 'Where are you going?' Birbhatti,[1] he was informed. 'Where is the harm, take him along,' the Sahib said.

Ahmad put his foot on the self-starter. The car hummed, shook and began to crawl. However, a gaunt-faced, wild-haired young man with a shaggy beard, a pencil in his right hand and a large register in his left, came and stood in front of the car. The car had to stop. The man bent towards the radiator and looked at it carefully. He straightened as he laughed, *hi, hi, hi*. He extended the pencil and register and spoke in clear English, 'Now then, my Lord.' Without waiting for a response or attempting to add anything further, he bent again, and after intently looking straight at the radiator, laughed and again repeated himself.

Perplexed, both Ahmad and Qureishi spoke at the same time, 'What do you want? Who are you?'

The man put his hand in his coat pocket, extracted and proferred an imaginary card, and asked, 'Do you think in English or in Urdu?'

Qureishi Sahib stayed silent but Ahmad answered immediately, 'Speak in Urdu, please. What does all this mean?'

'Good,' the man answered. 'Urdu it will be. These days, I am trying to present the eternal and living perspective on the ascending order of human thoughts. This means, I have distilled, purified and considered the essence of the individual and collective feelings, and inspirations of the entire world. I have it all...in this register. However, for the sake of my respected and honorable audience, this humble individual, that is Professor Daya Shankar Dube, will present to the esteemed crowd, with pure ecstasy and in all humility and modesty, the philosophy of the radiator, after diligent meditation, in brief.' He bent towards the radiator again.

[1] The British had established a wine factory (beer *bhatti*) at this spot. The factory was buried in a landslide in the nineteenth century and the place has since been known as Birbhatti.

'God save us! Who is this gentleman?' Ahmad said. Surprised, Qureishi Sahib was still silent, when the attendant at the petrol pump ran up and pushed the Professor Sahib away from the car. 'Drive away quickly, he is insane,' he said. Ahmad moved the car and when they passed the Professor Sahib, Qureishi Sahib noticed that the Professor only believed in clothing the top half of his body so his legs were not indebted to any *dhoti*, *pajama* or trousers.

The car drove on again. After running for a furlong on a straight road it turned left. A hundred paces later it turned right. Now the road began to wind and zigzag at each step as it ascended. The car must have taken a few more turns and twists when it took a particular turn and a cold gust of life-giving breeze blessed the car with its touch. And when the car took yet another turn and crossed a bridge, continuous, cold gusts started blowing…and then more, and in a minute, lo, the season had changed. The view changed and the world came alive again. Just minutes ago, when the ascent had begun, the large scorching stones implanted in the dry bed of sand and gravel on one side of the road, shone in the sun, emanating flames that dazzled the eyes. On the other side, far away, was the wall of the heaven-reaching hills. The living and dead shrubbery and the dust-covered wilting bushes beside the road sighed warmly and seemed to curse the dust-raising cars that passed them by. This changed within minutes. The car was now running between fresh, lively, swaying trees, verdant, pleased, foliage, wet slopes and rocks dripping with water. The constantly winding, looping road, caressing the open slopes, exalting the chasms and changing directions at every step, began to look like a light brown line on the dark slopes of the hills and the car began to look like a tiny bumble bee.

As the car twists and turns, its occupants are constantly rocked from side to side; those who are not used to this feel dizzy and start to retch. This ride was a new experience for the poor hill-dweller as this was the first vehicle he had ever sat in. Though he felt much better because of the cool air, the two and a half cans of water that he had drunk was now in tumult because of the turmoil in the car. This was also the first time the hill-dweller had been honoured by such an experience. When his mouth filled with water from the first spasm, he pressed his neck with both hands as an extra precaution; this gesture had the same effect that placing the palm on the mouth of a soda water bottle as soon as it is opened, has. When the water gurgled again with full force, it sprayed from his mouth on to the dials, meters and levers in front of him.

Ahmad immediately stopped the car and readied his fist but considered it inadequate so he bent down and picked up the car pump. Then he thought that would be far too severe so he threw it down, put one of his hands on his forehead and with the other on the steering wheel, sat there, a picture of helplessness. Qureishi Sahib had been lost in thought and now he was startled and angrily asked, 'What is the matter, ji?'

Ahmad answered tearfully: 'He is vomiting.'

Qureishi Sahib: '*Arey, Arey*, what is this?'

Ahmad: 'You invited this trouble. The bastard has soiled everything. Heaven have mercy he has even soiled my feet.'

Qureishi Sahib: 'Get him out, now, at once.'

Ahmad: 'Get out, you nuisance. Get out.'

At the place where the car halted to unburden itself of the hill-dweller, there was a small spring which emerged from between two rocks and, wriggling through wild strawberries, flowed as a stream over the leaves of a medicinal plant into the drain on the side of the road. Ahmad took water from this stream while he ate and spat out the ripe and raw strawberries growing there. He then cleaned the car. On the other side of the road, beside a very deep pit, the hill-dweller too removed his *pajama* and got busy in cleaning up. Nature was helpful in every way. The heat started to leave him every which way. Sound, excrement and vomit all began to flow at once. The car moved on while he was busy and once it had moved, the thought of the hill-dweller departed from the mind of the honorable Ishtiaq Ali Qureishi, the aristocrat from Badayun, forever. However, Ahmad, with his well-oiled, slicked and parted hair, wearing his hand-me-down silk shirt, kept silently cursing the mother and sister of the hill dweller. Then he too forgot about him for some time. The car reached the nineteenth milestone from Nainital. Across the bridge in front, where the road widened, another road branched off which, after winding a few times as it climbed through pine trees, reached Qureishi Sahib's bungalow about a hundred feet up.

2

Those in the car whizzed away and within minutes were in the mountains but our monkey was still walking under the trees on the side of the road. Her pace was slow but her tail was erect. At each step she found strange wonders of nature like *bidi* stubs, pieces of paper, scraps of cloth and cobwebs in the roots of trees; all of which she had to examine and scrutinize and a lot of time was wasted thus. It was not just these distractions that delayed her. Among the trees beside the road were many mango, *jamun* and neem trees on which were withering blossoms and emerging fruit. The monkey had to take care of these too. Because of her casual gait and these distractions, it was soon evening. While she was trying, by eating the bitter neem berries, to change the tart taste in her mouth produced by the *jamuns* and sour raw mangoes, a holy man with a tilak on his forehead, passed by her. He placed two fistfuls of roasted gram near the roots of some rushes and then, raising dust, tossing gram in his mouth, moved on. The monkey forgot about the heat of the loo, the neem berries and the dried fruit blossoms, and leapt towards the rushes. Two heaps of roasted gram awaited her there. The fare was delicious. Both her hands began to move. She began to examine them and put them into her mouth with both hands. The heaps of roasted gram began to disappear and lumps began to appear in both her cheeks which soon grew and began to hang like bags from her face. The roasted gram was now finished, although a few were hiding in the dust and the monkey, sometimes with her right hand and sometimes with her left, dispersed the mud and picked them out. It was then that another passerby appeared.

Even though the traveller was not much bigger than the monkey, he was a human and magnificent. He wore a turban of thick cloth with four folds in it, raw leather shoes with pointed tips and springy heels, and a tight well-starched *dhoti*. With half his face around the eyes covered with *kajal*, sniffing hard to draw up the stubborn snot that was bent on dripping down, a thick stick in one hand and a small bundle in the other, his eyes fixed on the monkey, he approached fearfully. Whenever the monkey looked at him, he would stop. Finally, he was alongside her. The monkey now lifted her head and looked closely at the boy. The boy stopped and lifted his stick. To test him, the monkey took a step towards him. The boy screamed at the top of his voice, '*Ho Dada, Ho Dada*!' The monkey did not need to know more and she was next to him in an instant. The boy turned speechless for all he could say was '*he he he*!' The monkey made menacing gestures. The boy waved the stick and still uttering *he he he he*, began to step back. In this confusion, the bundle on his head seemed to be frightened off its perch and tumbled down. The monkey ran up and caught it. The grandfather, whose help had been sought so forcefully, appeared, carrying a basket hanging from a stick. He put his basket down in the middle of the road and, with his bird-headed walking stick in his hand, ran towards the monkey, screaming, 'Oh your sister...! May your sister....' The monkey, with one hand, picked up the bundle that the boy had dropped, and moving on three limbs, ran to a tree. She stopped for a moment to crouch, and then with three leaps went and sat on the highest branch. The grandfather stood below the tree, waving the bird-head wildly while he loudly repeated, 'May your sister....' The monkey sat on top of the tree, and plucked out and ate the edible contents of the bundle as if nothing was happening. Then, from nowhere, appeared a huge monkey with a red bottom, who calmly and diligently got busy with the basket left in the middle of the road as if it were something that had been left especially for him. He bent into it as if looking for something he needed.

Dada Sahib now turned his attention from the monkey settled in her heavenly abode towards his basket. And when the large monkey could no longer bear the extremely disrespectful aspersions cast on his sister, he took what he could and limping on three limbs, went and sat on another tree. Since it was only a packet of tobacco that had fallen to his share, he smelt it and then scattered it slowly. When the basket, the grandfather and his three-feet-high grandson disappeared from view, and the male and female monkeys were done with their bundles, they descended. The male monkey speedily, the female one slowly because she was afraid. Once they were both on the ground, the male grimaced and attacked the female.

Actually, the male was no stranger; he was the female's mate and it was his darling baby that clung to her chest. He was a large-hearted, pleasure-loving, well-bred monkey, and therefore had another ten or twelve wives. All of them were a part of the band which was going to the hills for fun and recreation in the summer. During their journey, they had had to leave the female behind because of her untimely labour. Since the band of monkeys was moving slowly (as it should), the female had hurriedly taken care of the postnatal rituals and begun moving again. She was now near the rest of the monkeys and had run into the male who had been taking a stroll on his own.

The veteran gentleman was furious at his female, and his anger was justified: the untimely labour, her staying behind, the time it took for her to catch up, etc., etc. Growling and grimacing, he went to her and took her painfully to task. He even pulled her by the tail (which in human terms is like pulling the hair of a woman). The female apologized in every way she could—begged him with folded hands, explained her compulsions and problems, not through words but by shivering, placing her hand on her forehead and uttering '*qi qi qi,*' and when the cruel monkey still did not forgive her, she drew in her limbs and lay flat on the ground on her stomach, raised her head and stretched her lips till they reached her ears and started murmuring, *kich kich, kich kich, qi qi, kich kich, qi qi*. And when (God save us!) her tail was pulled, she urinated (getting thrashed is a horrible thing). Anyway, after much ado, the male's temper, which had kept boiling up, finally subsided. When relations between them improved a bit, the female followed the male to where the band of monkeys was encamped.

A hundred yards from the road, across the drain, surrounded by small and large bushes and average sized trees, stood the grand banyan tree with its flowing tresses and beard, supported not just by its huge trunk but by many other columns, looking, with its canopy of dark green leaves, laden with raw and ripe berries, like a multi-storeyed, magnificent castle. It was in this that the monkeys were staying.

How festive it was, what splendour and liveliness! Berries were being eaten, monkeys were playing; some were exercising, others wrestling and one was swinging from a branch. Another jumps from a branch and catches hold of his legs. Look! one upon the other, now both swing! The one on top lets go his hold and both fall with a thud, get up immediately and run away. One has scratched another and is now being chased. One jumps from branch to branch and another moves from leaf to leaf. One gentleman lies on a thick branch on his back, his arms stretched towards his head, enjoying himself. (If he were to turn on his side he would fall off.) A female is picking the lice off another male who is lying with his armpit exposed. Her mouth moves, *plukh plukh*. She swallows a few real and thousands of imaginary lice. Another female looks at them with envy and slowly comes closer. Hesitantly, she extends her arm and touches the male's back. She wants to find out if she would be allowed the privilege too, but no. The monkey, still on his back, grimaces at her. The scorned wife leaps and sits at a distance. The current favourite inches closer and her mouth works at double speed.

Two babies have challenged each other and are now wrestling. Their mother sits close by, knitting a sock.... Oh no! She is pulling apart the nest of a Jaya bird while proudly watching her promising sons. The sons were very young and they raised their arms, stood on their legs and got ready to fight. One of them lost his balance because of his disproportionately large head and fell flat on his back. The other stupidly pulled at his own tail, causing himself to roll over. Above them, another gentleman hanging by his feet over their heads, considered letting go any minute.

Since monkeys, like us humans, are concerned with only four things in life—being born, eating, procreating and dying—hence, among them too, must surely be some unfortunate, sad, lifeless ones, and so it is. One female moved around, hugging a baby which had been dead for a week. The baby's head had just fallen back and she was looking at it intently. (How must she be feeling?) An old female, many of whose grand and great grandchildren were frolicking among this band, was sitting on her haunches near the large tree. Her long arms were stretched out and rested on her knees. Instead of a shiny fur coat, long, scraggly hair hung all over her. Under hanging eyebrows, her eyes were sunk deep in their sockets. For hours she sat thus, staring at one spot, thinking. Sometimes, a dry leaf fluttered past her ear and she moved her head to the side, let it fall and continued to sit there.

Do not tease me, you star of spring, for our ways are different
You have playfulness on your mind while I sit here helpless.

Life! Full of pleasure and rapture! An enchanted childhood, free from care; the intoxication of youth! Are you bestowed on us so that in our last days we scourge our bent backs to shreds with memories of you? Oh no. I have begun to speak of myself. I sit on a bare cot, smoking a *huqqa*, with spectacles on my nose, a pencil in my hand and a register with yellowing pages in front of me. I scratch my beard as I get lost for hours in writing imaginary tales.

Memories. Memories of childhood draw on the script of life that has gone by, and I am startled as I watch this movie. I sit on a cot, writing tales of wonder. I am talking of the old female monkey. O you monkey, old, female monkey, you are fortunate! Your aging, tired limbs, your fading sight, your sinking heart make you sit thus for hours, but so what? At least your mind is free of memories of the past and worries about the future.

You are lucky, for I, for the sake of earning a little money, am writing with quivering hands of how the male monkey, with his female in tow, rejoined his band. There was immediate commotion. Those who were on the trees came down and those on the ground climbed up the trees. Their grimaces and the sounds of *qu qu* from all around, expressed two contrary emotions—hate and love—and wars broke out because of these. Children were safely protected by arms. However, peace and tranquility returned as quickly as the violence had broken out and the female monkey formally rejoined the band.

The band stayed in the tree all of that day, fed on its berries, and drank water from the stream. They spent the night there and moved on the next day. They left the road and headed towards the closest hill to the north. They fed on flowers and fruits, destroyed nests, and broke branches as they jumped, fought, confronted and grimaced at each other as they climbed, day after day. In ten days they had reached the height of five thousand feet and the walnut trees on the road to Nainital, between the eighteenth and nineteenth milestones. The monkeys were not comfortable in the climate at this height and it seemed they might turn back immediately. But the tasty raw walnuts and the blueberries held them back for a few more days.

The rains had not yet arrived in full force at this altitude though there were scattered showers. The weather was still agreeable. The days were very pleasant but the strong gusts of wind at night made the nights uncomfortable for the monkeys. They would brace themselves tightly, utter *koon koon* and sit close to each other, waiting for the cold of the night to pass. As soon as day broke, they forgot about the night's discomfort and busied themselves again, enjoying their holiday in the hills. In this delightful climate, the monkeys, lively by nature, became even livelier. Every one was happy and merry. Each felt the urge to be naughty; even the old female felt a faint stirring of life. Sometimes she would sit on a slope, dislodge a rock or two and watch it disturb other small and big rocks as it rolled down. Even the newborn of our female—whom we last saw near the well and on the road, sucking on the same teat for hours as he clung motionlessly to his mother's chest—had first come alive, and now leaving his mother's arms, started moving and jumping a bit. But he was still very little and each part of him was out of proportion—a large head, a small stomach to which were attached four arms and legs and a tail—all of which looked like reeds. On his wrinkled red face were black-rimmed eyes and the hair on his head was parted. Once, he stopped feeding at his mother's breast, jumped out of her lap and sat on his haunches. The mother, who was sitting three feet away from the stream under a big boulder, plucking and eating the tri-foliated leaves growing under it, remained as she was but extended one arm, caught hold of the baby's tail and pulled him back towards her. This went on for a long time. Behind the female were the slopes, and on these, far and wide, among the trees and bushes, other monkeys were peacefully engaged. A clever little monkey often came close to her and tried to tempt her baby into playing with him. The last time he had tried this, the female even snarled to scare him off. But the naughty monkey did not give up and was once again stealthily approaching the female from behind. The little baby was standing upright on two feet and looking covetously at the vagabond kid, over his mother's shoulder. He wanted to make friends with the other young monkey. He tried unsuccessfully to jump over her shoulder, then went under her arm and with small leaps headed towards the other young monkey. The mother, still plucking at the leaves, suddenly noticed his absence, turned around and saw the naughty monkey tempting her baby further away. She was angry and leapt towards them but she was only a yard away from her baby when she stopped where she was. She heard '*Dana na na dan dan....*' Oh, what was that? Her ear drums seemed to split. Her heart began to pound *dhar dhar, dhar dhar, dhar dhar*. She jumped onto a rock, then onto a tree and then jumped and went higher. The female had left her baby behind and was now on the top of the tree. The other monkeys began to run in every direction. A man emerged from behind a rock and came near the baby. The baby was lying flat on the ground, grinning and making sounds of *kich kich, kich kich*. The female jumped from the tree onto the rock. Ahmad fired his twelve bore gun again, twice, *dan dan*. The female began to jump from the rock to the tree and then back on to the rock. Two large monkeys made frightening sounds of *khu khu, quq, khu khu,* though they couldn't make up their minds whether to attack or retreat.

The entire band of monkeys now began to scream *khu khu, quq, khu khu*. As Ahmad bent and picked up the baby, a yellow car glided up and halted near the rock. Ahmad, with the baby, jumped into the car and Qureishi Sahib, who was at the wheel, whizzed them away. All this must not have taken more than ten seconds. Now, whatever the monkeys did mattered little. Scores of them ran growling after the car but there was nothing but the empty road before them. Even the fumes of the car had dissipated. The crazed mother ran from monkey to monkey screaming *khu khu*. Each of the monkeys, their ears stretched, their eyebrows raised and the hair on the back of their necks and their backs still bristling, answered the female with *khu khu*. It seemed that each one was saying, 'Aunt, why did you not do something yourself?'

The aunt did her best to incite them to be brave by growling, grimacing, shrugging and raising the hair on her back, but in vain. When she saw that they would do nothing, she ran as fast as she could in the direction that the car had gone. Some young ones kept her company for a while but they soon returned.

My readers must be tired of hot plains, dusty roads, running cars and leaping, screaming monkeys. So I will introduce them into a peaceful, relaxed, luxurious, spacious, beautiful, well-ordered house furnished with chairs, tables, couches, sofas, durries, carpets, screens, curtains, pictures, mirrors, vases, flower pots and scents.

Qureishi's Sahib's home, Firdaus Cottage, was not one of those buildings that stand on a main road to exhibit their dignity and magnificence. Instead, like those individuals whom an excess of wealth raises above the need for self-adorning and self-praise, this majestic building, calling itself a cottage, stood hidden amongst pine trees, far away from the city, as if its being was in no way indebted to the city or the road. It could take care of all its own needs. And this was true. In its garage, apart from Qureishi Sahib's simple Buick and his Begum's Rolls-Royce, were two common Fords which like slave boys were always ready and waiting to run errands to Nainital, Kathgodam and Bareilly. In the grounds, trees laden with apple, pear, plum and apricot stand around a smooth cement tennis court. All around are flowers in pots, bushes, trees and creepers, experimenting with scent and colour while absorbed in the delicate task of being decorative. Hidden at the back is a kitchen garden with tomatoes, peapods and so on; beyond it, the well-ordered servant's quarters some distance away. Externally, the house made no effort to look pretty. With its sloping tiled roofs it looked like a pile of expensive red tiles, surrounded by glass windows and enclosures whose heptagonal and octagonal window panes protruded and peeped out from behind a veil of flowering creepers.

In the small porch-like verandah, which creepers and hanging pots had turned into a fern house, sits the fair, elegant-minded, dainty-tempered, meagrely built Firdaus Bano working on the crossword in the *Illustrated Weekly*, with the help of a thick dictionary. Between her and the telephone sits Qureishi Sahib's widowed sister on a low three-legged stool, as scared of the telephone as she is of her sister-in-law. She is stitching a light blue dress. In the middle of the verandah white liveried servants are silently laying the table for evening tea. At the other end of the verandah two mothers (or two mothers-in-law), opposites of each other in every way, sit on the same couch.

Firdaus Bano's mother and Qureishi Sahib's mother-in-law is fair, simply dressed, white-haired, thin, given to laughing for no reason, devoid of intellect, content and happy with life. She is the single, undisputed owner of this household but neither is she aware of her rights nor would she want to assert them.

The other lady—fat, ugly, bejewelled, a bundle of colourful clothes, grey-haired, eyes blackened with eyeliner, eyebrows arched, and mouth twisted—is Qureishi's mother and thus Firdaus Bano's mother-in-law. She is a guest here but looks for every opportunity to assert her proprietary rights. She issues orders and when they are not carried out, gets annoyed, even enraged. She suspects every one of insolence and defiance. She ruled the roost in her husband's lifetime and now, though he and his wealth have forsaken her, her haughtiness has not. Right now, she is staring angrily at the south Indian ayah who is rocking the baby in a cradle at the edge of the verandah, even though she had specifically instructed her not to bring the baby out because of the cold. The ayah, in assertion of her ayah-hood, brought the baby out for fresh air and kept repeating, 'I know how to look after Baba better than you, Bibi. I'm not new at it. I have worked for grand English ladies. Bibi, you know nothing.'

The Bibi retorts, 'Get lost. May your face catch fire, you fat outcast. How dare you be impudent, you progeny of English ladies....'

The widowed girl could no longer keep quiet. Irritated, she said, 'Mother, let her be.' And then turning to her sister-in-law she said, 'O bride, have a look. Is this all right?'

Firdaus Bano replied angrily, 'Older sister your calling me bride does not sound nice. I have so often told you not to. Why don't you call me by my name?'

Kulsum (the sister-in-law), said with a sheepish laugh, 'Forget it. It was a slip of the tongue. Take a look at this. I hope it is not tight.'

Firdaus Bano took the shirt from her and looked at it. She neither praised it nor did she pull a face. 'Yes, it is fine,' she said as she handed it back. Just then the car returned.

Qureishi Sahib got out of the car, took the baby monkey from Ahmad and enthusiastically approached his wife. 'Here, Begum,' he said as he pulled out the baby monkey, which was trying to hide under his arm, and held it towards her. The baby monkey began to cry *qain qain*, showing all its teeth. The Begum Sahiba threw down the magazine, gathered her sari and headed for the hall. 'Please leave it there, just keep it away,' she said as she went. Uncertain whether to disappear inside or come back out, she halted.

Qureishi Sahib's mother said, 'Good. Son, you have done the right thing by bringing it. I've often told you that the presence of a monkey near the baby keeps all sorts of illnesses away.'

Qureishi Sahib replied, 'Yes, mother, you did tell me that and Ahmad too told me that with a monkey around, the atmosphere is cleansed. Look, I have finally brought one today.'

He once again extended the baby monkey towards his wife. The wife once again indicated that she might turn and run and hide inside the room.

Qureishi Sahib's mother-in-law spoke, 'Son, take him to the baby. Let's see what he does.'

The ayah (now shielding the baby, both arms outstretched): 'O, no, no. The Baba will get scared. It will bite the Baba.'

Qureishi Sahib's mother: 'Get lost, you witch. She now wants to play mother!'

Firdaus Bano: 'Come on, mother! Of course he'll be scared.' To her husband she said, 'Just keep him away. Won't his presence be of help even if he is kept at a distance?'

Firdaus Bano, and perhaps even Qureishi Sahib, would never have tolerated the presence of a monkey in their house, let alone near their baby. Born eight years after their marriage, the baby was the result of thousands of prayers and was also sickly and weak. He seemed afflicted with consumption from birth. Both parents doted on this child. Though he was only a month and a half old, dozens, nay, scores of toys had been bought for him. The doctor visited every third day to take a look at him. If anyone suggested anything they could do for the child's benefit, they would abandon rationality and act like the ignorant. This was the reason the baby monkey had come into a human abode. Let's see how this turns out.

3

Instead of cleansing anything, the baby monkey started making a mess everywhere from the moment he arrived. When given milk, he would put his hand in the cup and try to lick the milk dripping off his fingers. He couldn't eat anything that was hard.

When given overripe bananas or *khichhdi*, he ate a little and spread most of it around him. Everyone had opinions about his diet, the place to keep him and his training, but these opinions were given from a distance. The responsibility of looking after him fell on the poor sister-in-law as if she was born for the job. The sister-in-law, in the same way as she had taken on other unpaid jobs meant for maids, accepted this too with a sheepish grin. After a few days of experimentation, a large bottle with a nipple solved the problem of feeding him milk. A small cot had been ordered for him which he used only when he lay down to drink his milk or when he wanted to defecate. He was constantly looking for opportunities to get on to a chair and rest on its arms. When they gave up on him, he was moved out of the room into the attached verandah. Here, he found a convenient perch on the bars of the grill. Even though the pitch-dark ayah would smack him every time she passed, at least there was open air here. He could see the trees in front of him and behind them, the hills. He would sit for hours, scratching his waist, watching the scene.

It was from these trees on the hills that one day his mother emerged. From the trees she jumped into the tomato patch and then crept forward until, in three leaps, she was on the grill and hugging her baby to her breast. The separated were united. The baby clung to its mother. Hearts met silently. The mother never told him of the nights and days she had spent searching for him in the hills, moaning *ou ou*. Nor did the baby weep and tell her about being beaten—beaten for not drinking his milk, for not lying on his cot, for smearing *kheer* all over, for refusing to wear a *kurta* or for urinating and defecating. All that happened was that the two pounding hearts met. The baby, while he sucked on her milk, looked up and the mother looked down on him in silence, and their souls merged. In the fading light of evening, lightning flashed across the sleeping greenery. The baby clung closer to his mother and the mother hugged him back. The day was ending. It was a dangerous time—a time to settle down for the night. The monkey decided to move to the trees. She had reached the ground when the baby was pulled from her chest while he screamed *ki ki, ki ki*. She climbed back on the grill. She clasped her baby again and started to descend when the baby screamed again and held the rope that was tied to his waist. (Ohhh, the poor baby was tied!) The mother descended again and the rope pulled back the baby again. Lightning flashed again in the gathering darkness. Thunder reverberated across the hills. In front of her was a thicket of trees and above, dense clouds. Both mother and baby pulled again and again at the rope. Then they jumped down to the verandah and walked around; then the monkey climbed up on the grill again with the baby clasped to her. She tried to leave again but the rope tightened again. The baby struggled and was pulled back. In the growing darkness and as the thunder grumbled, the monkey—driven crazy by maternal instincts—circled the pillar to which the rope was tethered, went through the grill, climbed up and jumped down, went around the pillar and through the grill again, but she couldn't get rid of the rope. Instead, the rope got entangled and tightened further until it was impossible to move. When he struggled, it tightened further. The rope now cut deeply into the baby's waist and he started screaming loudly. The mother's heart was being consumed by dread, fear, panic, horror, confusion, agitation, despair, helplessness and love. It was now completely dark and it had begun to rain. Suddenly, there was a sound. The frightened monkey screamed *Khi* and jumped. Someone switched on the light. Three bulbs lit up the verandah as if it was still day. His mother's leap caused the rope to tug at the baby's waist. He was crying *ki ki, khi khi* when the door of the room opened and the ayah began to scream, 'Aayi, aayi Moongey, aayi aayi Moongey.'

The worshipper of that unattainable, imaginary and faithless god of fortune and plenty, Qureishi Sahib's mother, ran in, scolding the ayah, snubbing her daughter and rebuking her daughter-in-law.

Deprived of fortune and plenty but scavenging off it, Qureishi Sahib's sister ran up, avoiding the ayah, fearful of her mother and scared of her sister-in-law.

Oblivious of the good sense that accompanies fortune and modernity, the simple mother of Firdaus Bano also came; pleased with herself and the world, she stood behind the rest.

The monkey was grimacing as she stepped backwards till the servants came running. She snarled a last time before she jumped onto a walnut tree and, jumping from tree to tree, got lost in the forest. Later at night, as she sat crouched on a branch in the cold and the rain, the inhabitants of Firdaus Cottage began to dine in the warmth beaming from the radiator and the soft light filtering through lamp shades. The ayah, baby in arms, sat on a stool near by. The baby monkey was tied to a rope attached to the latch of the cupboard near the door. They began to eat as they conversed and laughed. The ayah spoke and the Sahib laughed. There were jokes, laughter, mild taunts and snubs, objections followed by more jokes and laughter. And while they talked and laughed, the baby monkey continued to pace as far as the rope would let him.

Much later, when dinner was over, when the radio too had finished speaking, when the baby monkey had been locked up in the bathroom, when the family in their bedrooms and the servants in their quarters were fast asleep, Qureishi Sahib as he turned over in his soft bed of silk and wool, heard two sounds from far away. The first was the sound of the female monkey who suddenly missed her baby. She cried *oou oou* as she moved from tree to tree. The other sound from some unknown person came from farther away, two thousand feet below, near Birbhatti. Loudly, the voice proclaimed 'Now then, my Lord.' Without any hesitation, the hills answered 'Now then, my Lord…then my Lord….'

Shivering at the thought of the dark night and the cold gusts of wind and rain, Qureishi Sahib drew his warm silken quilt tighter around himself and went back to sleep.

The female monkey was sighted again near the house over the next three days. Sometimes she was simply near her baby and at other times, feeding it. She did no one any harm. She fed the baby a few times a day. This seemed to have become her sole preoccupation because the band of monkeys had failed to convince her into leaving with them when the monsoons arrived. The female was left alone among the trees. She would jump around, feed herself on fruits and leaves and then feed her baby. Once, she found pieces of *roti* and some fruit lying close to her baby and she ate them. Another time, while she was feeding the baby, a woman opened a door close to them and threw out some pieces of *roti*. The female monkey was startled, left her baby, jumped off the grill and stood two yards away, her ears pulled back, her lips pursed and made threatening sounds of *khu khu*. She stood on her hind limbs and realized that food had been thrown at her. She came back and sat on the grill and, taking extra precautions, wrinkled her ears, jerked her head and continued to make threatening sounds. When the probability of danger faded and she was convinced this was a friendly gesture, she descended and began to eat the *roti*. From then on, she often found food left for her.

In a few days, the monsoons set in with full force. It became very cold and fog covered the hills. The monkey was already getting something to eat so she attached herself to the house. Here, she was protected from both cold and rain. There were also fruits on the trees and vegetables in the garden. Her child too was close to her so she settled down and as was her nature, she started eating, pulling out and destroying fruit, flowers and vegetables. When her stomach was full, she even began to examine the house. Sometimes, she would topple a vase or upturn flower pots, pull the curtains or carry away cushions from the hall. To add to all this, while her child would only defecate in the radius allowed him by the rope, she was free to scatter turds all over the bungalow. Soon after they decided to be hospitable to her, the inhabitants of the bungalow got fed up and started thinking of ways to get rid of her. Bi Amman (Qureishi Sahib's mother) and the ayah began to blame each other for being too friendly with the female monkey. Firdaus Begum blamed her sister-in-law and cursed her for it. The sister-in-law, with self-conscious giggles, began to look for new little ways to flatter her. Firdaus' mother treated everyone as equals and while she agreed with everybody, began to display her strangeness even more overtly. The day the mother monkey defecated on the dining table and then decided to clear a row of wine glasses off a shelf of the whatnot which came crashing down, no one could bear it any longer. Orders were issued to Ahmad and Qureishi Sahib himself, in his silken *shalwar-qameez* and soft soled shoes, began to fire at the monkey who was now playing hide and seek on the roof of the house. Firdaus' crazy mother, her fingers stuffed in her ears, first began to plead with everyone on behalf of the monkey and when everyone disappointed her, she tearfully appeared before Qureishi Sahib and begged for mercy, 'Son, it is wrong to kill a monkey. It has never been considered good and I'm very superstitious about it.

May Firdaus live, her child is still young. Son, don't kill the monkey, it will be highly inauspicious.'

The result was that Ahmad was summoned, his valorous passion was calmed down, and he was told that the monkey was not to be killed but that he should keep his gun handy and fire in the air to frighten her away. Every time the monkey appeared, she was to be scared away. With humans losing their wits at the sound of a twelve bore gun, what chance did a monkey have? In two days, dread overpowered her maternal love and she started avoiding the house.

The monkey was alone in the bitter cold hill chasms and caves, amidst heavy rains, biting winds, fog, dripping trees, and wet grasses. Her band had returned to the plains without her and her baby had been taken from her. The weather was hostile too. The food available to her was strange and meagre. The monkey would sit for hours, hungry, on a wet cushion of thick ferns, watching the silent clouds swirling around her. Eventually, the fog would swallow everything around her and the helpless monkey, with no clue as to what was happening and why, would dispel the gloom that enveloped her heart by letting out long drawn out sounds of oou oou.

Alas, we were separated the moment we embraced
The wounds of the heart had not yet healed.

Inside the house, the baby was traumatized by being separated again from his mother and was restlessly awaiting her return. When hope gave way to hopelessness he too started expressing his despair with sounds of *oou oou*. A desperate, heart rending would escape his heart, whether in the silence of afternoon, the quiet of evening or the stillness of night. The filth had decreased and the damage to things had been considerably reduced but the household was exasperated by these sounds which never stopped, from the moment they awoke to the moment they went to sleep.

One day, when some friends and political leaders were over for a tea party, these sounds brought up the subject of the baby monkey. The doctor was present, and said, 'When kept in captivity, the germs of tuberculosis develop very quickly in monkeys' chests. A monkey should never be kept in the house.'

Both Qureishi Sahib and his wife panicked the moment they heard this. They immediately declared that they would release the baby somewhere far away the very next day. However, among the guests was a delicately built, not too educated but very broad-minded young lady called Miss Sheila who, like many young people today, was attempting to combine the two extremes of Vedic meditative practices and modern thinking. She pleaded that she be given the baby monkey, to which they readily agreed. The progeny of an animal thus left the degrading life at Firdaus Cottage and achieved a godlike status at Oak Lodge because the fairy-like, delicate minded, daintily built Sheila, daughter of Gobardhan Lal Dube, ICS, had grown disgusted with the brazen, drugged gaze of the *pujaris* at the Hanuman Mandir at Talitar and had brought this living Hanuman to worship at home.

The splendid Oak Lodge had a drawing room, dining room, side rooms and parlours furnished in elegant English style with expensive things, but also had a room on the red walls of which were pictures of *rishis* and gods surrounded by eyes. The walls and floors of yet another room were washed and scrubbed before sparkling brass buckets and *lotas* of water were placed on well-washed small stools. This room was used for bathing and there was another for applying *tilak*, where elders of the family, bare-chested and wearing the sacred thread, immersed themselves in devotion, prayer and meditation. In other rooms vermillion, sandal wood, tulsi leaves, coconuts and other items were made ready in neat thalis for *puja*. There was a verandah where thin white dhotis, hung length-wise, fluttered in the breeze and where glasses made unclean by use or utensils which became absolutely impure once they were eaten from, were collected. There the dog would lick them until enough had been collected for the water-drawer to scrub them with mud and cow dung and make them clean again. Attached to this verandah was a small room where a peg was driven into the floor close to a wall. This room was plastered with cow dung. Here, the educated, open-minded, aficionado of fashion, devoutly religious, extremely modern, supporter of progress, with the mind of a leader, Sundar Devi Sheila, a devotee of Hanuman, having just emerged from her bath, hair wet and ripening youth wrapped only in a silk sari, with a small *lota* in one hand and a *thali* full of *puja* items in the other, came to worship Hanuman. The baby monkey was busy trying with both hands to press a brass plate in which he had been served food, on his head. He immediately turned to her. The plate from his head fell and rolled, clanging, on the floor. All his attention now on Sheila, he started kicking the *thali* with his feet. Calm and respectful in her faith, she sat before him and got absorbed in prayer. However, the monkey was interested in the offerings much before they were offered. He came forward as far as the rope would let him and stretched out his hand but couldn't reach the *thali*. Sheila moved it an inch farther away. The monkey took two semi-circular strolls along the radius defined by his rope and during the third round, suddenly turned his head towards the peg, stretched out his body, extended his leg and caught hold of the *thali*. Immediately, Sheila grabbed the *thali* from her end. They both started to tug at it. On Sheila's innocent face were signs of amazement, anger and fear. Colour appeared on her cheeks and worry on her mouth, and the sari slipped from her chest. 'All right, take it,' she said, pushing the *thali* towards the monkey as she stood up. For some time she glared at the monkey who was busy with the vermillion and flowers; then, moving like a cobra, she crossed many rooms with lightning speed and reached her well-appointed room, where she stood before a picture of Hanuman flying with the island of Lanka on his palm, folded her hands, closed her eyes and with extreme helplessness and humility began to pray for her husband, Professor Daya Shankar Dube (to whom she had been married as a child but had never met).

Different people with differing hopes get entangled in all sorts of worldly cares. They then devise various schemes, innocent of the unalterable intentions of the real God and occupy themselves in worshipping all sorts of gods. Coincidentally, the inhabitants of Firdaus Cottage too were involved in worship at the same time when Sheila was lost in her worship of Hanumanji. At this very time, having descended 1500 feet from Firdaus Cottage, these believers were offering supplications and praying for favours at the shrine of Ajab Shah in Birbhatti. Outside the low wall of the shrine, Qureishi lay half reclining in the rear seat of the car, half-awake, a cigar in his mouth, letting out small puffs of smoke. In the shrine, his fairy-like wife sat teary-eyed, her legs folded under her, her arms raised, praying for the health and life of her beloved, weak son. On one side of her were two large trays of sweets covered with a silken cloth, absorbing the spirituality emanating from incense burning in earthen saucers. On her other side, next to the grave, lay her child, flailing his arms and legs. Behind them and facing the child, sat Ahmad, ineffectively snapping his fingers to distract the child. Next to the incense sat her mother, trying to do the impossible—to gather the blessed fumes with both hands and to rub them on her face. At the head of the grave—where, in an arched, smoke-blackened niche sat a *diya*—sat Bi Amman, arms half raised, her eyes rolling, mouth agape, waiting for dusk to fall and the lamp to be lit. She prayed silently, 'Shah Sahib, diminish my son's love for his wife and increase his love and respect for me.'

Next to the door, in the courtyard, stood the sister-in-law, laden with her sister-in-law's fur coat, the baby's quilt and her mother's shawl. She stood hugging them, her eyes closed as if she had just met these dear ones after years and was warming her heart with their affection...but no Sir, she too was praying silently, 'Shah Sahib, somehow put the thought in my sister-in-law's mind that she fix a monthly allowance for me so that I can escape these vexations and live on my own in our house in Badayun.' Next to the door, but outside the courtyard, stood the infidel, south Indian ayah who was forbidden from entering, showing all the white teeth in her dark face. All were preoccupied in their own thoughts. The keeper of the shrine, Shah Waliullah Sahib, the perfect saint, sat leaning against the door of the shrine room, busy with his prayer beads. His luminous, wheat-complexioned face shone from the oil rubbed on it; above was a domed net-cap, a square black beard below it and on both sides coiled tresses twisted into hollow reeds. Having graduated through all the stages of the spiritual quest, he seemed lost in contemplating the divine. But the moment Firdaus Bano finished praying for blessings and turned her face to each direction, he became alert. He got up, wrapping his prayer beads in his hand, went to the moss-covered earthen pot kept in the corner and with the tin tumbler attached to it by a chain, he drew some water, rinsed his mouth thrice and came and sat near the tray of sweets with his legs folded under him. More fumes arose from more incense. After he was given five *annas* for lighting the lamp, five for the incense and a hundred rupees as an offering, he prayed to the saint. A *chadar* was offered for the grave and a thread tied as a reminder of the favours sought; hands were raised again in supplication as they left. Shah Waliullah Sahib, pinching dead an impudent louse that had strayed from his tresses on to his blessed face, went towards the room again. He got a pen, ink and paper and sat down. He put the paper on his knees and while he recited prayers, began to write invocations to God which were to be worn as amulets.

It had been raining continuously for the last few days. It had stopped in the afternoon but now it began to rain again. The south Indian ayah standing outside began to make a commotion, 'Aayi, Aayi, Memsahib, water falls.' Everyone got into the car in a hurry. The Shah Sahib blessed them again for the last time by leaning into the car and blowing on the infant. Qureishi Sahib started the car and Ahmad followed in the other car. Passing the small market of Birbhatti, the two cars came to a brief halt because a bullock cart was blocking the road. There, on the roof of a house, they saw Professor Daya Shankar sitting, tied to a chair. He was saying, 'Now then my Lord, so this is the reason why you become the world of the being of those who damage the country while we who get consumed by anxiety keep gaping at this Satanic behaviour and become the critics of men's sins. Today those imprisoned in India are going in a motor car to sing the virtues of a half-critic while manifesting them in a mental void.' Having said this, Professor Sahib bent down, examined the cane tuffets and again saying, 'Now then my Lord,' continued his lecture.

The bullock cart moved and the car proceeded. The people in the car were extremely surprised at what the mad man had said—little did they know that in their absence another mad man was saying even more incomprehensible things at Firdaus Cottage.

This man, Abdul Hakim, was the nephew of Qureishi Sahib. In Ahmad's room, he was busy packing his shaving kit, crumpled ties, crushed suits and worn out socks as he recited poetry, cursing his fate and the omnipotent One.

Can we claim departed pleasures from the heavens?
Is the highway robber our debtor because he stole from us?

How well said, uncle Ghalib! Surely you suffered many blows of fate or you could never have written this couplet. You say—it is futile to consider the robber our debtor because he stole from us.Well said, my friend! You call the old man a highway robber! Very well, he may not exactly be a highway robber but how appropriate was it for the decider of our fate to assume the title of the Compassionate and the Merciful? He closed his eyes and apportioned whatever he felt like to people and we are helpless before him. But Sir, if you claim to be Compassionate and Merciful, you should be ashamed of yourself. Is this what you call mercy and justice? I should have ruled this bungalow. This house should have been mine. The villages in Bareilly and Badayun, the buildings in Bombay, the cash in the banks should all have been mine. I am the son of the eldest son but am today employed for a salary of rupees seventy five and six annas per month and even this bloody job is in trouble. What would have been the harm if father had lived just a year and a half longer? All right, Allah Miyan, if you so desperately needed to call him to you, you could have called my old grandfather before him. If the old man had passed on just ten days earlier I would not have been considered *mahjub*.[2] What injustice! Today I, a *mahjub*, roam around in rags while my uncle

[2] That which is hidden. According to the Shariah, a person has to be alive to inherit, which means the child of a man who dies in his father's lifetime cannot inherit his grandfather's estate.

lives like a nawab. I have been hanging around here for a week as a menial, hoping for a small recommendation from him. The day I arrived there were house guests who had come to play bridge so I stayed here with Ahmad in his small room. But once the guests left, no one thought it fit to ask me to move into one of the other rooms. I asked him for the small favour of putting in a word for me, but he's afraid he might lose face if he does. Of course, he must not lose face even if it means I have to starve. Shame on such an uncle, and shame on me for coming to him for help. Look, he promised that today he would meet Mr Ilford about the matter but he's gone off somewhere else. And where? To worship at graves. If worshipping the old man doesn't get you anywhere, how will worshipping mounds of mud help?'

Hakim continued to curse, as he packed his belongings, and got the gardener to carry them to the road as they were drenched in the heavy rain. He climbed into one of the lorries passing by and left. On the way, he continued to recite the couplet.

Can we claim departed pleasures from the heavens?
Is the highway robber our debtor because he stole from us?

4

Insha Allah Khan Insha[3] is a comic. He said:

'The finger dances immersed in the divine world.'

This is simple vulgarity and pure obscenity. In reality, this is what the divine world where Allah resides looks like—if the mind could scan seventy thousand years to the east, seventy thousand years to the west, seventy thousand years to the north, seventy thousand years to the south, seventy thousand years above and

[3] An Urdu poet, 1756–1817.

seventy thousand years below, it would find nothing. There is nothing but a vacuum. And in the midst of this absolute emptiness and nothingness, if there is anything, it is a small timepiece which continues to tick.

Centuries and eons have passed but the clock of the divine world continues to tick.

Centuries and eons will pass and the clock of the divine world will continue to tick.

When planets collide, when worlds are smashed, the clock of the divine world continues to tick.

When an egg falls from the nest and breaks, and the bird flutters around, chirping in distress, the divine clock continues to tick.

Indifferent to the drunk's tuneless singing, hungry orphans' cold sighs, widows' sobs and beauty-chasing young men's guffaws, the clock continues to tick in the divine world.

The Divine is laughed at. It is even abused and mocked when divine attributes are ascribed to animals, stones and mounds of mud. Yet, the divine clock continues to tick.

What glorious indifference, tick, tick tick.

Listen to it, Sheila, listen, Firdaus Bano. Listen, oh Abdul Hakim.

Tick, tick, tick.

In the dark night of the gloomy jungle, in the rain and the biting cold winds, the drenched female monkey sat on a wet, dripping tree. A channel overflowing with rain water roared somewhere close by. The sound of the gushing water echoed off the surrounding dark slopes and in between these simultaneous sounds were squeezed the frightened, long-drawn out cries of the female monkey. Darkness, rain, strong gusts of cold wind, the roar of flowing water and the rippling sound of mountain streams; along with all these echoed the long helpless sound of *ooo ooo*. And then again *ooo ooo*. But this time after the painful *ooo ooo* there were sounds of *khi khi khi*. What is this? Is someone tearing her apart? Is someone stabbing her with a spear? *Oo oo khi khi khi khi*! What is the matter? She is surely in pain. Something hurts her at intervals or she is very distressed.

In the darkness, animals start moving. A few squirrels came down from the trees and began moving through the grass and plants towards the western slopes. Leeches and rabbits were moving too. Leaving their perches, birds fluttered and flapped their way in the same direction. The female monkey sat where she was, still making frightened sounds of oo oo oo. Then, bewildered and uttering *khi khi khi khi*, she climbed down the tree, branch by branch. Making sounds, she moved in the other direction. Where is she going? To Firdaus Cottage? Yes, that is where she is going. Hiding in the darkness, she is moving towards the cottage. A wild cat approached and passed her, but she did not stop. She finally reached Firdaus Cottage which was fast asleep. There was complete silence. Nearly all the lamps had been put out. In the rooms there seemed to be a few faint lights. The female monkey came to the verandah where her baby used to be, and started making sounds of *oo oo*. When there was no response, she began to run this way and that, making sounds of *khi khi khi khi*. She made sounds of *oo oo* at the window panes, against the closed doors but she heard nothing. Ah! Where is the baby monkey? In panic she ran around making sounds of *khi khi khi khi*. She climbed on to the roof. She jumped down from there. She went around to the other side of the house. She made sounds of *oo oo* all around and when she could find no way of getting inside the rooms she again went around the house. The worried, anxious monkey who had been running around suddenly spotted an open window. She jumped into it and then on to a chair. From there, she leapt on to a table and then onto the fire place. A vase fell with a thud. She saw another open door. She went through it into another room and there too she scrambled around in panic. She entered a third room just when the choked screams of Firdaus Bano merged with a heavy, dull, frightening roar rolling across the hills.

This frightening sound had originated thousands of feet below and was gradually increasing and spreading over miles. Now the rooms were echoing with this sound. The walls were shivering. Firdaus Bano had been woken by the sounds of the female monkey and the rest were woken by Firdaus Bano's screams. They were now terrorized and witless, shivering and frozen wherever they were. Driven by maternal love and only by it, the monkey roamed around, searching for her baby and reached the cot of Qureishi Sahib's only son. Love and only love, in which there can never be any feelings of revenge, envy, jealousy or hate. She was looking for a balm for her aching heart. She needed a baby to clasp to her heart. She found a baby. What kind of a baby? Whose baby? How did any of this matter? She tugged at its clothes, flung away the quilt and hurried along, clasped the human baby to her chest. The ayah screamed loudly. Holding the baby firmly, the monkey leapt down. She jumped this way and ran that way. Some of the people had got up and others were screaming. Some were running around. Some more doors had been opened. Hearts were thumping, the walls were shivering. Not only the house and the trees but even the hills were shivering.

The monkey emerged from the house with the baby. What was she to do now? The hills were falling. The land was slipping and along with it, houses, gardens, trees and the jungles above and below. The situation was changing in fractions of seconds. The land had split in places. Upright trees were now awry in the places where they had once stood. Qureishi Sahib's house shivered, shuddered, fractured and like a coward, crumbled into a heap. Its rubble raced downwards, followed by tumbling multi-hued trees. Thousands of maunds of stones, lakhs of maunds of slabs raced down. They mingled and raced down together. Thousands of huge trees, crores of maunds of rubble, lakhs of maunds of rocks tumbled over each other, rolled over, shattering and getting shattered, crushing and getting crushed themselves, rolling and destroying everything that came in their way. And in all the uproar—in the darkness and amidst the lakhs of rocks tumbling down and the rapidly slipping slabs—the female monkey, enveloped in dust, ran on three legs (with the fourth she was holding the baby), avoiding the smaller stones and jumping on the larger ones. A tree, monsterlike, with hundreds of arms, approached her, sweeping everything before it. The female monkey jumped on to it and then from branch to branch. Tons of slabs, rocks, trees and mud were continuously falling from above. The entire slope of the hill, from the peak down to Birbhatti, had slipped. The habitation of Birbhatti was now buried under a few hundred feet of rubble. Huts and houses, rich and poor, saints and mendicants, all were buried. The scattered remains of Firdaus Cottage too were buried under yards of rubble while more continued to pile up on it. In this calamity and confusion, the female monkey continues to jump from rock to boulder to tree, and then on to rocks that bury the tree. She uses only three of her limbs and with the fourth she clasps the baby to her chest. She is constantly moving. She jumps on to anything that might crush her and when this is threatened with burial, she leaps on to whatever is about to cover it. There is so much dust in the darkness that it is hard for her to breathe. And the noises, O lord! It seems like the end of the world....

After the destructive night the sky smiles innocently. On the silent hills, dawn breaks. The clouds have cleared, the fog has lifted and the winds have stopped. A few birds are chirping. The habitation of Birbhatti lies asleep, cold, covered in three hundred feet of mud and stone. Ahead, the dark, intoxicated mountain looks like it is yawning, stretching open its one and a half mile wide, two thousand feet long mouth. It is a long yawn and will last for some time. It will take five or six hundred years for thick jungles to grow again to hide this mouth. Right now there is just vacant land where Birbhatti lies covered under the earth. And this uneven mound will stay as it is until it is washed away into the Bay of Bengal or is covered by forest and made into a green spot to picnic in. People who have never heard of Birbhatti will come here, stroll around and enjoy themselves. But for now it is a mound of mud, rock and boulders from which, here and there, stick out the broken branches of large trees. At places, there is evidence of human activity too. At one place, lies a stone marker for furlongs from the road above, showing the unlucky number of seven to the sky. At another, a frightened end of corrugated tin sheet peeps out of the earth. In the middle of the mud, for no reason or purpose, the wooden pillar of a house stands half buried. On its tip is entangled a ragged piece of cloth which flaps like a pennant. It seems that the land slip, having achieved its aim, has planted its flag of victory. Quite a distance from this flag, the gravely wounded female monkey, still clasping the human child to her breast, is in the spasms of death. It is still all around. The birds are chirping. The days are getting brighter.

A voice is heard from a distance, 'Now then, my Lord,' and the mumbling sound draws closer. Professor Daya Shankar Dube, wearing only a shirt and a jacket, approaches giving a lecture. He reaches the pillar and stops. He looks at it intently and addresses it, 'Now then, my Lord, the exaltation I have achieved from making your acquaintance today cannot even be matched by the joy of divine revelation. I therefore congratulate you because it is a huge mistake to believe in the non-existence of the conflation of thought and speech. This humble creature therefore requests you to stay where you are while I move on.'

As soon as the professor had moved away after his intellectual greeting to the flag, a hill-dweller emerged from behind a boulder, where he had been hiding for some time, watching the monkey with the baby. He took the baby from the dead monkey in his arms and walked on. Peace and quiet prevailed again. The corpse of the female monkey lies there. No one weeps over an animal's corpse. Oh, the only son of Qureishi! The heir to millions, I weep over your corpse. You too are dead. The one heir to Qureishi's houses, land and villages, is now dead. The child whose life the female monkey saved at the cost of her own is now the child of an animal because it is the hill-dweller who will raise him. He will live and grow up but into another life where thought processes will be different, patterns of speech will be different, ways of life will be different, social manners will be different. He will be a hill-dweller, unaware of his property, ignorant of his religion, unaware of his culture and will look at his own class from a distance, with fear. His original associates will avoid him as if he is not even human. You are now a half-civilized hill-dweller; they are educated, broad-minded people.

It would be indeed surprising if it is the human intellect that has raised humans from bestiality to a position where they become deputies of God.

Is man really of sound mind?

Not as a Hindu, or as a Muslim; nor as a Qureishi or a hill-dweller, become human, only human. O man, take a look at yourself in this mirror, it is the mirror of wonders.

I jabber all sorts of things in my madness
God, I hope no one understands anything I say.

Tick, tick, tick, tick, tick tick, tick, tick, tick, tick, tick.

A Nemesis for Every Tyrant

The residents of the jungle around the river Mala awoke and began to stir in the deserted *sal* forest as the day ebbed. The jungle, which had appeared empty of animals, began to bustle. Silence fell once the birds settled down for the night. Some daylight remained and because it was not completely dark, it was still early for the jungle creatures. Only low-caste animals like pigs, *chital* and blue bulls appeared, and moved around fearlessly, looking for food. At this quiet and peaceful time, a huge, mad, obdurate, malevolent pig dug at roots with his snout, grunting, and chasing away any animal that came close. To the west of the forest, because of the heavy *sal* trees and the thick undergrowth, it was completely dark. To the east, the rays of the setting sun were still visible because this was the edge of the *sal* forest where, close to a net of creepers, stood a hedge of thorny bushes. Below this, after another stretch of trees was the wide bank of the Mala River where shallow mire and swamp was hidden by an expanse of elephant grass which stretched out brown and still. On the banks of the river, or shall we say in this ocean of grass, were dense clumps of jungle which were beginning to fade from sight in the evening light.

The wild boar heard sounds from this grass. His snout stayed buried in the mud but his ears twitched. The sounds stopped. After a short pause, the pig had just buried his nose in the mud again when sounds of *khis, khis, khisaak* came from the grass. The boar stopped digging at a root, and without moving his head turned his entire body around with a jerk so that he was now facing the Mala River. He curled his tail up into a curlicue and stood still. Animal sounds continued to emerge from the tall dry grass. By listening to each particular rustling sound, the short-sighted boar could usually figure out which animal was approaching. He assumed that an insolent blue bull with his females was again coming his way, since several of them had already bothered him that day. Taking a couple of steps at a time, jerking off the sparkling white stems that were wrapped around his snout, he moved forward. In front of him was a net of thick, bare, intertwined stems of wild creepers which had climbed up tall trees, trailed down to the bushes below and then climbed back onto the trees again, hanging like swings. There, under a hanging creeper stood the original inhabitant of the swamps and elephant grass that grew on the banks of the Mala, the mighty wild buffalo. He stood, holding his thick horns aloft like branches. He was waiting for his females who were following him at a leisurely pace.

Calves, young adults and females appeared, one at a time, at the mouth of the narrow track in the elephant grass. They stopped and looked around before leaving the grass cover and, keeping track of their young, they gathered behind the male. The male wild buffalo is the largest of the hoofed animals in the forest and very conscious of its build and strength. This arrogant bull flared his nostrils, cupped his ears, turned them forward and vigorously switched his short flat tail. He was irritable from having been made to wait. He also could not figure out what ill-mannered, audacious creature dared stand in his path.

Ahead of him, hidden in the small bushes and grass at the edge of the salt forest, stood the silent, startled boar who was invisible to the buffalo. Because of his short-sightedness, he too couldn't see the buffalo. The pig was convinced that he was heading towards blue bulls and when he heard the sounds of the females, he dismissively made spitting sounds—*khuq, thuk, thuk*—and leapt towards them. He emerged, swiftly and noisily, from the short grass and was just fifteen yards away from the buffalo when he realized his mistake. The powerful buffalo stood fearlessly before him, holding high his horns with their lance-like gleaming tips, and looked at him with contempt. Blue bulls and deer could be threatened and scared away. But a wild buffalo! A buffalo! *Tauba, tauba*, never. The pig halted in his tracks, turned around, snorted *thu thu thu*, took to his heels and kept running.

The proud buffalo, strutting silently, moved forward, leading the way. Behind him came the calves and the healthy, sleek females, wriggling their buttocks and shoulders, kicking their feet, arching their necks—enthusiastic, hesitant, jumping, leaping and playing with each other. Thus, one of the many flocks of wild buffaloes of the Mala moved into the *sal* forest. Ahead of them, *chital*, blue bulls and pigs cleared out of their way. The buffalo herd, under the strong male's protection, began to move casually and fearlessly towards the east of the *sal* forest. After walking a mile and a half, they moved to the salt lick deep in the jungle near the tarred road. The calves and females surrounded the ditches, lowered their necks and began to feast, licking the salty earth. The male stood apart for a while, surveying the surroundings. Having satisfied himself on all counts, he moved slowly towards the salt and had just lowered his head when from the Mala end of the *sal* forest came soft sounds of *purr, jhurr, phurr*. The entire herd, including the male, started and looked in the direction of the sound. The night was dark and the dense jungle even darker. The light was perfect for forest animals. The buffaloes saw a dark, mountain-like elephant displaying two white tusks, his trunk lifted to trumpet his arrival.

For a few minutes each buffalo stood still as stone, not even moving their eyelids as they looked at the black monster. Then they all started to run at the same moment, randomly at first, but then the females formed a circle around the male as they ran.

In peaceful and happy times, the male moved ahead of the herd, investigating possible dangers. Now, however, as they ran helter-skelter, ignorant of the lay of the land, it was the females who risked their lives, escorting the male progenitor as they ran to safety. Such is the tradition of all the hoofed animals of the jungle. On this occasion, once they had reached the motor road, they turned southeast, against the wind, so that they would be forewarned of any dangerous enemies hiding in the dense forest ahead.

When the buffalo herd had run away, a male elephant made the soft sound of *peenp par rororo, pa, pu* to inform the herd following him that it was safe. Soon after, dark mounds, with fan-like ears, waving trunks like pythons began to appear. The herd included males, females and the young. These rolling hills broke branches, pulled out bushes, waved the broken branches in their trunks and on their pillar-like legs moved forward, crossed the motor road and entered the bamboo forest. Breaking bamboos and crushing bushes, they recklessly moved towards the delicious patch of paper reeds hidden in the jungle. They could soon smell these reeds. One male stepped forward to scout. He put his head out of the dense bamboo grove and greedily looked at the field of reeds, rippling in the wind. The tip of his uplifted trunk turned in all directions as it checked out various scents. The fan-like ear twitched to catch sounds. When the scout had reassured himself in every way, he uttered a soft bugle call of *peenp pa ro ro ro, pa pu,* indicating to the herd that it was safe. In return came the angry growl *oa aaoon wa aw wa aan khun* from a tiger. Earth shook, bushes shivered and trees trembled. The elephants ran back madly, crushing more bamboo.

It was past midnight and the moon, peeping through tall trees dripping dew, scattered its fading light on the reeds in the shallow, dried-up lake surrounded by tall, dense, still, silent, dark jungles. At one end of the patch, a sandpiper fluttered, calling *teet teet, titeee, titeee, titeee, tit tit, titeee, tit ee ee, tit eee*. The moment the tiger roared at the idiotic elephants, the sandpiper, with a last call of *titeri, tit, tit, titee, titee*, flew north and disappeared. The ten-foot striped tigress sauntered gracefully into the reed patch but stopped suddenly.

There, a hundred or so feet away from the jungle, among the trampled reeds, her two young ones were attacking a half-dead female buffalo. One stood next to the buffalo which was on the ground, his front claws buried in her waist. The buffalo continued to make efforts to rise but he pushed her back down. The second cub held her thick neck in his small jaws and jerked at it with all his might, emulating an adult tiger who in two jerks separates the vertebrae in its prey's neck. Earlier, the tigress had already broken the buffalo's neck and had left it half-dead for her cubs to kill. Its head hung down. But like a rooster whose neck has just been slit, the buffalo struggled, moving her head and wanting to run away. When the cub on her back diverted his attention to her rump, the injured buffalo made another attempt to rise. She rose to a sitting position.The cub that had been clinging to her neck was now hanging from it but he lost his grip and fell. He moved back four yards and crouched, waiting to leap once the buffalo moved. The cub at the buffalo's rump had his teeth and claws buried there. As soon as the buffalo staggered to its feet, this cub moved his teeth to the inside of her legs and thighs and was now clinging to her like a lizard. The cubs were the size of a dog and their weight was nothing compared to that of the buffalo. This last rush of blood incited her death spasms.

The lamp flickers brightest before it dies at dawn.

Drenched in blood and with more flowing from her nostrils, head rolling from side to side on her neck, the buffalo kicked her hind legs and tried to run.

The tigress stayed where she was but contracted her body. Her chest and stomach touched the ground and she was ready to spring at the buffalo if need be. But just then her second cub appeared like lightning and for a moment seemed suspended in air. His hind legs and tail were stretched straight backwards and his front legs were parallel to his neck. He shot like an arrow released from a bow and landed on the running buffalo's back. A loud sound—the buffalo was again on the ground, its limbs splaying out. The two cubs, avoiding the kicking hind legs, grabbed her again. The tigress heaved a sigh of relief. She stood up erect and with great pride moved slowly towards them.

However, to this reed patch surrounded by jungle, the wind blowing from the west carried a fresh scent followed by sounds. The tigress' paw remained raised as she paused mid-stride. She stood still, not even moving her head.

The light wind bore the smell of raw sugar and also the whispering sounds of heavy feet. The insolent, audacious elephants were approaching again. The queen of the forest was enraged. Lightning shot from her eyes and her claws turned to curved daggers. The curled tail straightened. Her fierce mouth bent towards the ground. And then she roared. Heavily, the roar spread across and scared the jungle. The tigress was mistaken. This time it wasn't a herd of elephants but a lone male. This one-eyed, deceitful, crazy *mustt* elephant with one and a half tusks, was obstinate and built like a mountain. Despite having lost half a tusk in a fight, he had defeated every other elephant. He roamed around, thirsty for blood. Within his massive frame, eleven feet high at the shoulder, was contained unimaginable strength coupled with over a century of experience. Nature had bestowed on him tyranny, cruelty, mercilessness, shrewdness and deviousness. His mighty build was matched by expertise in how to use his strength. Casually and indifferently, the tip of his trunk in his mouth, he heard the tigress' fierce roar which had terrified the forest. From his left eye, now empty of its eyeball, continuously flowed dark tears which had permanently stained his cheek. His other, working eye, he now squeezed into a small ball which rolled around a few times as he looked at everything.

The one-eyed elephant turned and soundlessly moved away from the tree. He let out soft sounds of *pu ru ru* and then walked in a semi-circle away from the tree till he reached the west side of the lake. He softly walked along the river bank and waited behind a very thick tree.

The tigress, unaware of any of this, entered the *sal* forest, carrying the heavy, dead buffalo by its waist, very much as a cat carries a mouse. However, the neck and feet of the buffalo were dragging and both cubs constantly tugged at them, trying to drag them in different directions. Irritated by their untimely antics, the tigress growled softly at them as she walked through the sparse undergrowth between the tall *sal* trees. Suddenly, she saw four tree trunks move and then speed up towards her. Before she could put down the buffalo corpse and look up, her ear drums were shattered by a loud bellow. Her gaze kept rising higher and higher as she looked up at the elephant.

She saw a strange dark monster with an endlessly long trunk emerging from a head high up in the air, standing firmly before her, challenging her to a fight to the finish. In front of the tigress was her kill and beside her were her two inexperienced cubs. The danger was imminent and present. She was furious. Her veins throbbed. She contracted her rump and before you knew it, it was either a furious flame or an audacious bolt of lightning that sprang from the ground and reached the yards-high trunk of this monstrous enemy. Suspended in air, the tigress tried to get a good grip on the trunk so that she could chew it off the jaw before she tore it to shreds with her claws. But the trunk moved like a flying snake—this black beam of death moved past her face to her ribs, where with a thud it landed, carrying the force of a few maunds. The tigress fell to the ground. The elephant sprang towards her, sending out a kick meant to annihilate her. However, there was nothing to kick. Having sprung with tremendous agility, the tigress was now trying to bury her teeth and claws into the yellow hide on the elephant's shoulder. The elephant shivered and then shrugged with such vigour that the tigress lost her grip. Again she fell, three yards away. Then, a sixteen-maund paw landed like a steam hammer which would have reduced her to an imprint on the earth, at the spot where she had landed. The tigress had moved as fast as thought and was now chewing on the elephant's rump. Again, the elephant tried to shrug her off but this time in vain. The tigress had driven her dagger-like teeth and lancet-like claws inches deep into his thick hide. Despite being agitated by the pain, the elephant halted for a moment. Then casually he walked around in a semicircle. His only working eye did its duty and spotted a huge tree. The elephant moved slowly towards it and when he was close to it, he jumped swiftly. The four-foot wide tree and the elephant weighing hundreds of maunds formed a clamp which crushed the bones of the tigress. A life-ending scream escaped her. The jungle echoed.

For a long time the one-eyed elephant continued crushing the tigress against the tree. When he was satisfied he began kicking around her flattened corpse. He then held it under one foot, tore apart its limbs and flung them in different directions. His anger had not yet cooled, so he began to kick the torso like a football as he moved towards the east of the *sal* forest. He reached the edge of the forest where clearing had begun and arrangements for sawing the trees into sleepers were being made. Some trees had been felled and a few carpenters had come and casually begun their work. Since the site was not fully functional, the one-eyed elephant did not find much to destroy here except a few warehouses. He trampled on these and then flinging some hay on his head and stuffing some in his mouth, he drew out one of the poles from what was once a thatched roof and walked on to feed in the cultivated fields.

As he did every night, after walking for ten to twelve miles, he left the grazing grounds. Around three in the night, the one-eyed elephant emerged from the jungle north of the village Pipariya. Outside the jungle, the miles-long barricade of thorny branches and bushes was no obstacle for him. With his trunk he pulled out yards of the barricade and flung it aside. Then standing in a field of yard-high wheat, he selected plants, wound his trunk around them and with a jerk pulled them out—roots and all. He shook these clumps in the air and then hit them against his front legs to get rid of the earth still clinging to them. He then folded them, stuffed them in his mouth and began to enjoy himself as he chewed.

As luck would have it, a short distance away, the watchman sleeping on the scaffold-platform woke up. He heard sounds of *chur mur jhur*. He thought that pigs had entered the field. Daybreak was close and it was cold. The man lay wrapped in a quilt and blanket. He stayed as he was and called out, *dhu aala la la, dh aa aa,* and began to snore again.

The wicked elephant fell silent when he heard this. For a while he stood with half a bunch of wheat plants in his mouth and the rest in the tip of his trunk. Then he spat out the plants, extended his trunk as if to trumpet, raised his ears and slowly began approaching the platform. When he was close to it, he again stood still. Then, a single step at a time, he walked to the platform. Near the platform, he stopped and listened to the snoring. He moved to the platform as slowly as before and placed his trunk on it. Wrapping it around the man's legs along with the quilt, blanket and thick sheet, he pulled him off with a jerk, waved him around in the air twice and then holding the bedding with his foot, started ripping it apart.

The man was no longer in the bedding. He had been flung out like a pillow from its case and had fallen far away. Buddal, son of the hunter Kalua Pasi, was a young man but had spent all his life in the jungle. Since he was nine or ten, he had been guiding hunters or had grazed his animals in the forest. His five senses had doubled to ten. As soon as the elephant wrapped his trunk around his legs, some unknown sense warned him of grave danger. He held his breath and relaxed his body; when he emerged from the encasing of his bedding and landed with a thud on the wet, watered earth, he let out no sound. He lay still just as he had fallen and started to listen intently to the sound of ripping cloth. Then he heard a satisfied hiss and feet moving through the crop. When the sound faded away, he raised his torso on his arms and in the faint light of dawn saw the evil-hearted, monster-like elephant enter and disappear into the forest.

While this athletic, sturdy young man was still prone on the ground, torso raised, looking over the wheat crop at the elephant, about fifty steps behind him, on the boundary of the field stood Jhulli, another lad from the village, watching the fun. The same age as Buddal, he was weak and devious. Jhulli mocked him patronizingly, 'O brother, come to me. Come here. Come on. Come here, I'm waiting.'

Buddal turned his head and looked at Jhulli. He was enraged. Despite the severe pain in his waist, he immediately answered, 'Just wait. I'm coming,' and stood up quickly. They walked towards the village to inform others.

The brave Buddal managed to reach the village. His waist was massaged and fomented with heat. He was well in a few days. But he had been humiliated for no fault of his own and for this there was no cure.

Major Boast had spent some time in Africa and since then, his beloved fiancée Louise would, at the club, smile and look intently at others as she retailed stories of his exploits. Major Boast felt it incumbent on him to tell tales of having hunted fierce animals in the endless forests of Africa. These stories made his audience shudder; their hair stood on end and their imaginations ran riot. And this happened regularly. Once, when he had finished telling an audience of eight or ten, among whom were two ladies, his story of an elephant hunt in which six elephants had trampled and taken apart two of his gun-carriers and four coolies, a mild-looking young man who had been sitting silent, stood up and drew from his pocket, a folded page from *The Times of India*. Carefully straightening it out, he said, 'Take a look at this. It's an advertisement from day before yesterday.' He read out the advertisement placed by the Conservator of Forests of the United Provinces, which announced a reward of five hundred rupees for killing a rogue one-eyed elephant in the Pilibhit division.

The result of all this was that one day Major Boast, along with his six guns, four servants and enough provisions to be loaded on six bullock carts, disembarked at the Mala railway station, leading his white fox terrier on a leash and addressing his own servants as Indian dogs. Acting on instructions from above, the forest guard was waiting for him along with coolies and bullock carts. The luggage was loaded at the station and unloaded at the bungalow in the jungle, where the gentleman settled down comfortably at a leisurely pace. All day, cans of asparagus, sardines, sausages, fruit salad and cream were opened, emptied and thrown away. Sandwiches were made. Footmen ran in all directions to get milk, eggs, fresh fish and loaves of bread.

Major Boast kept himself busy with urgent chores such as reading the newspapers, answering mail, shaving, grooming his hair and bathing frequently and changing his clothes many times each day. His day also included frequent meals. Despite being so busy, he went out to hunt for two hours every morning and evening. Often he shot jungle fowl that he found foraging in the fields or a *chital* peeping out of the forest. Eight days passed thus. During this period he even shot a black partridge. He also managed to have a look at elephant footprints, over a month old, in a field four miles away. As far as the hunt was concerned, perhaps this was about all that Major Boast did. Showering curses of 'damn fool' on his personal servants, forest guards and railway employees, the Major left for Bareilly for a break of four days. However, Buddal had heard that a red-coated, red-faced Sahib was staying at the bungalow to hunt. He still carried his grudge against the elephant. The next morning he left home early, a spear on his shoulder and walked along the Mala River for miles, looking for elephant prints. When he returned home in the evening, his father asked, '*Arey*, where were you?'

'The Sahib who is staying in the bungalow to hunt has hired me as a guide. He hunts fowl and deer,' Buddal answered.

In the hope that the one-eyed elephant would once again return this way during the hunter's stay, he would set out every day to look for elephant footprints. Finally, on the fourth day, four miles away from the village, he found traces of the one-eyed elephant. Here, he had fed in a field at night, had crossed the mile-wide forest at night and walked into the Mala where he would spend the day in some island of trees before he headed out the next night in a different direction. Buddal ran back to the village the moment he found the traces. In the village he saw the landowner's mare. Hurriedly, he made a saddle of his blanket and raced to the forest bungalow. When the galloping mare reached the bungalow, it was ten in the morning. The Sahib was about to leave with three coolies who were carrying all the essentials needed for an elephant hunt—guns, bags, thermos flask, binoculars and camera. Buddal bowed low, his hand touched the ground before he raised it in salute. He informed the Sahib that he had found the elephant, that there was no time to be wasted and that they must leave immediately. The Sahib, however, spent half an hour asking many questions. Among these were: 'How many elephants are there? Is the one-eyed elephant among them? What is the jungle like? Are there any strong trees on which a man can stand and take aim? How far do we have to go?' Buddal had taken one look at the hunter and his equipment and had guessed that he was an officer. Impressed by his powerful guns, he gave him some correct information, invented some details and convinced him to leave immediately. The Sahib got on to his mare. A 32/40 bore rifle was given to Buddal and he was told how to load and fire it. Two others carried a matching pair of double-barreled 450 bore express rifles. The group left, the men walking both ahead of and behind the mare. Soon they began to run. Before they had gone a mile, Buddal had started walking beside the Mala, leaving the village behind to their left and he was now leading them towards the jungle. There were still three miles to go when the Sahib lost patience. Angrily he asked, 'How much farther is it?'

The Sahib had been under the illusion that at the most it would be a matter of a couple of miles. He expected to find the elephant standing like a black buck, waiting for him to take aim. The Sahib, used to firing ranges, would bring him down in a shot. Things had turned out very differently. After crossing many hurdles, what did they reach? The footprints of the elephant. Now it was time to enter the forest.

The Sahib became agitated and began to assert himself and ask questions. Buddal, once again, lured him on, 'We have done it. We are almost there. We have got the bastard.' Eventually, one of the two men was sent back to the village with the mare and they all began walking. Buddal led the way and the other man followed the Sahib. They began to walk fast. They crossed one patch of *sal* forest and then another. A third patch began but the search did not seem to be ending. They did not seem to be even close to the elephant.

At first the *sal* forest was clear of undergrowth. Then came bushes and grass that grew a foot or two taller than them. Now, under very heavy *sal* trees, they were walking through bushes much higher than them. They could not see beyond three or four feet. Major Boast was now in an awful fix. He could go no further, nor could he return. At every step he imagined a trunk appearing from the undergrowth and grabbing him. To make matters worse, Buddal was soothingly assuring them that they were very close to the elephant.

Mercifully, the jungle ended. Ahead, the wide banks of the river Mala, covered in brown grass, were dotted with clumps of dark green tees. Elephant grass rustled below the banks. The jungle behind them seemed dark. From it came sounds of *kut kut, kit kit, kut kut;* the sounds of a carpenter. The day was drawing to a close as it was two in the afternoon.

They stopped to catch their breath. The extremely red-faced Major Boast frequently wiped sweat off his face. He cast hateful looks at the grass in front of him and the jungle behind him. He took out a flask of brandy from his hunting bag, put it to his mouth and took a few gulps. He took a long breath and then downed a few more gulps. He then took out a cigar and lit it and only after he had taken ten to twenty puffs was he ready to move again.

This time when they set out, Buddal made himself very clear. He told them that the elephant would be in this clump of trees to which his footprints had led them. He warned them to be careful. Once again, Buddal led the Sahib while the other man followed. The Sahib held one of the loaded 45 bore rifles and the coolie the other. They began walking on grass trampled by the elephant. The path was dry in some places, wet in others and swampy in yet others. It was so tall and dense that they were swallowed up by it. It seemed as if they had dived into muddy water and were swimming below it. They could not see anything on either side, or for that matter, above them. They managed to cross this ocean of grass. They reached the forested island, as expected, lush with ferns and flowers. But it was so dense that the Sahib refused to go further. Now that it was certain that the killer elephant was in this small patch of forest, his mind would not let him go further. His heart too could be heard through his shirt made of woollen sun-proof serge which had cost eight rupees a yard. He planted his legs apart and firmly stood his ground.

He stood the two double-barrelled rifles against the tree in front of him. He cursed his fate. Then he cursed himself. Then, in English, he bestowed countless abuses on Buddal. He then drew out his brandy flask and cigar. While he was taking long puffs on his cigar and small sips of brandy, Buddal had nothing to do but look for the elephant's footprints which were as large as grinding stones. He moved from one to the next, staring at them. He did not intend to go far, but was only looking at the prints because he had nothing else to do. He traced the prints for about fifty yards into the forest when he saw them turn around towards the river. Buddal continued to follow them till it occurred to him that he had wandered too far and should return. He therefore walked away from the footprints towards the river. As soon as he got to the open sandy bank, his heart missed a beat. There, in front of him, were absolutely fresh footprints of the elephant, showing that it was now heading towards the Sahib. Buddal estimated that the elephant would now be about a hundred yards away from him. Immediately, he pulled down the lever of the 32/40 bore Martini Action Winchester rifle and assured himself that it was loaded. He then snapped the lever back in place, held the gun in both hands and ran. When he emerged from behind a bamboo clump, he saw that the Sahib, his eyes closed, was puffing at the cigar. And between him and the Sahib, hidden in the jungle, he saw the elephant approach the Sahib.

The devious elephant, very much like the careless tigress, was moving stealthily under cover. He was just a few steps away from his goal when Buddal let out a frightening scream to warn the Sahib. The one-eyed elephant turned swiftly and charged like lightning at this new, screaming enemy. Buddal was left with no option but to fight. 'Shoot him, Sahib, shoot him,' he shouted as he lifted his own gun, took aim and fired. He lowered his gun. He still had five live cartridges left in his fist. He reloaded the gun and fired again. He fired again after that but the bullets hit the six-inch thick bone on the elephant's forehead and glided off. Yet, this assault hurt and bothered the elephant. Buddal's last cartridge had emptied itself. He looked towards the Sahib and was disappointed. Then he turned and looked towards the edge of the grass and saw the Sahib disappearing into it. After that he saw nothing. He fell to a blow from the elephant and was crushed under three-foot wide feet. The bones, flesh and muscles of the young man were reduced to a dusty heap which the elephant kept kicking and plucking till it was nothing but unrecognizable scattered shreds.

The other companion of Major Boast had disappeared even before him. Only Major Boast knew of the difficulties he had to face to get back to the bungalow. He was happy to be alive. The bag, the ammunition and the pair of rifles had been left behind. The cartridges were not important but the matching 32/40 bore rifles were very valuable. He was worried about them so he decided that he would formally inform the Forest Department the next day that Buddal had absconded with them and the 450 bore rifle or that they had got lost. Strutting, screaming and abusing, the Sahib left for Bareilly.

Soon after he had left, Kalua Pasi, Buddal's father, anxious and worried, came to the bungalow, with a spear resting on his shoulder. For a long time he stared at the empty bungalow. Today, even the watchman from whom he could have made enquiries wasn't there. Eventually, heaving a long sigh, he turned back and headed straight to the forest.

He wandered from ten in the morning, his head lowered, breathing deeply, till five in the evening when he reached the spot where the group had entered the grass beside the Mala river, following the footprints of the elephant. The moment he saw the elephant's footprints, he also saw next to them the prints of army full boots and Buddal's spiked leather shoes. He sat down, held his head in his hands and started to moan. '*Hai Bhagwan!* Why this, my Lord?' he cried as he shook his head. He sat thus for some time. Then, suddenly, he stood up and saying, 'Buddal, Buddal! *Arey* my son, I'm coming,' he pushed ahead into the grass at great speed. The path of trampled grass was like a dark tunnel winding through yard-high grass, mire and swamp. Kalua kept his eyes fixed on the path. When he came across Major Boast's footmarks turning back, his mind lost its bearings. He instinctively called out, 'Buddal *re* Buddal, I'm coming, son.' His voice disappeared amidst the rustling grass.

Kalua now began to run in the grass like a man possessed. He reached the edge of the forest and was about to enter it when he suddenly turned to the prints on his left. He must have walked ten more steps before he stopped, amazed.

In front of him was a patch dug up by the feet of the elephant. All around were stains and splashes of blood. Also scattered around were pieces of a human being, caked in blood and mud, stinking and covered with flies. The thin bent barrel of the gun stuck out of the ground. A little further away lay two leather shoes and the broken butt of the rifle.

This sight converted Kalua Pasi from a father into the experienced hunter that he was. For the moment he put aside the fact of his son's death and began to think of the circumstances in which he had died. Carefully and very slowly, he examined each mark and everything else he found there. One by one, he picked up five empty brass shells of the 32/40 bore rifle cartridges from a spot near the largest blood stain. Then he pulled out the bent barrel of the rifle that was impaled in the ground. He dusted it and when he looked into it, he found the empty shell of another cartridge. Like a true hunter, he applauded. 'Well done, well done! He stood his ground and did not run. He ran out of cartridges yet he stood his ground.'

He then began to walk in the footsteps of the elephant. He reached the spot where the elephant had turned his attention away from the Sahib and towards Buddal. Here he noticed that when the elephant had turned left towards Buddal, he had not stopped directly in front of him. Instead, he had gone further to the left. He had then turned back and realigned himself to face Buddal. Even then, as he moved towards Buddal, he had moved right side first. Kalua mumbled to himself, 'He does not have a left eye. He sees only with his right one.'

He then began to wonder which way the elephant had originally been headed. When he looked, he found the Sahib's bag and a double barreled rifle leaning against a tree. Then he found the Sahib's footprints. He also found the cigar that had dropped from his mouth and the brandy bottle that had fallen from his hand. He checked the rifle and saw that it was still loaded. He went through the bag and in it was a hunter's knife, a few bottles, an unopened tin of cigarettes and many other such things to which he paid no attention. He counted the cartridges and as an extra precaution reloaded the rifle with fresh cartridges.

By now it had become dark. Kalua sat down on the roots of a tree, leaned against its trunk and began thinking of how his son had died. In a little while it was pitch dark. Dew started dripping from the leaves of the tree and from the faraway outer forests across the Mala River emerged the cries of *chital* and the bellows of wild buffaloes.

At first light, Kalua took the rifle, speedily set out along the elephant tracks and kept walking at the same pace until evening. Yes, he did stop a few times when he came across a drain or ditch full of water where he had a drink. Apart from this, he did not stop for a moment.

The elephant had left that patch of forest and crossed the river.

Kalua walked in the jungle towards the north. In the evening, he bent down once again to check the elephant's prints. He took a pinch of the elephant's droppings, rubbed it and shook his head in disappointment. The elephant had set out twenty hours before him. These tracks were old and it was getting dark again which meant that Kalua would have to postpone his search and spend the night. And it was at night that the elephant would head out again and the distance between them would increase. But what was Kalua to do? He climbed a tree and spent the night on it. He hadn't eaten all day. A state of drowsiness descended on him and lasted all night.

The next morning he set out again. Now he was no longer keeping track of the patches of jungle or their boundaries. Nor did he have any idea how much distance he had covered. He walked unsteadily because of hunger and fatigue. But he was possessed by his search for the elephant. His heart was aflame with the desire for revenge. He still had the strength of determination which drove him forward.

At one in the afternoon he bent down and picked up some more droppings of the elephant. These were soft and moist inside. Kalua was sure these were droppings from that very morning. He wondered if the elephant had chosen some place close by to spend the night. In this hope Kalua began to move faster. He was now walking through dense reeds and therefore had to move forward on all fours because growing amidst the reeds were small thorny bushes of catechu. As Kalua moved ahead, the slush increased and turned into a swamp. All this convinced him that the elephant must have chosen some place just ahead to spend the day and would stay there till evening. Now, he had to reach the elephant as soon as he could because once it was dark the elephant would set out again.

Once the swamp ended, bushes began which were denser and thornier. To traverse these he had to crawl on his stomach. At one point, as he emerged from the bush, he saw the elephant tracks cross his path.

Kalua heaved a sigh of relief and followed the trail. He found droppings again. When he touched these, they were warm and fresh. He now began to walk on the left side of the footprints because he knew the elephant could not see with his left eye. As he moved ahead, he increased the distance between himself and the footmarks. Because of the density of the forest, he often had to move back to the right to examine the footprints more closely and see the direction they were taking. In this state, Kalua was aware of even the faintest sounds. His eyes moved constantly. In each fist he had an extra cartridge, and he carried the loaded rifle in front of him. He moved alert, avoiding bushes and constantly searching. Once, when he was again approaching some of the elephant's footprints, he heard the sound of branches crackling. Now, he began to move slowly and came within twenty steps of the elephant. The elephant was standing at an angle, breaking branches off a tree. Kalua fired twice in quick succession at the elephant's temple. The elephant panicked and ran. Kalua began to make a huge din as he chased him. After some distance, because of the din Kalua was making, the elephant stopped and turned towards him. Kalua stood still in front of the elephant. As soon as the elephant charged, Kalua moved swiftly to his left and shot twice in rapid succession and from very close range at the elephant's temple because of which the elephant went down on his knees and then, with a crash, fell to the ground. Kalua fired two more shots at the fallen elephant and then leaned on the gun as he began to bend over and fell to the ground. His limbs had given up but the fire of revenge had not yet been quenched. He took the gun, emptied it of the used cartridges and tried to drag the bag towards him. He wanted to reload the gun and fire some more. But the gun fell from his hand and he fainted.

However, the next day when Amir Ahmad, the forest guard, along with two other watchmen, found him, Kalua was sitting on the elephant's stomach, crying, with his head in his hands. He was arrested and tried for illegally using arms. It was also announced that he deserved the reward of five hundred rupees. In the course of the trial Major Boast had to appear and, with his head lowered, give details of his hunt. Whenever the Major was about to begin boasting, the Deputy Commissioner—who was Louise's father—would immediately stop him and start questioning Kalua Pasi about his investigations because Louise wanted Major Boast to be compelled to admit his cowardice in public. And it was to hear this that she was present in court.

Shirin-Farhad

Had it been you or I, we would have pleaded in pitiful tones:

'Come to the terrace, I'm waiting for just a glimpse.'

But in the dark, lonely lane, all that Farhad could do was to call to Shirin at frequent intervals, in a beseeching, drawn-out tone: *aao, aao* and as he waited for Shirin, the pathos in his *aao*[1] increased till it became *aaoo.* Only when *aaoo* became *aaaooo* did madam Shirin stroll on to the rooftop. Springing and crouching, with great style she contracted herself as she sat down and looked down at Farhad in the street below.

Farhad let out a sigh and said, '*aaaooo.*'

And indifferent Shirin answered, '*mian aao.*'[2]

The suitor, however, had vowed never to set foot in her house after he had been hit with a racket the other day. His back still hurt. He kept inviting Shirin to come down to the street but where was the need for her to do so? She sat where she was for some time, listening to his *aaaooo, aaaooo.* Then she got up, invited him once with *mian aao*, and gently disappeared.

How could Farhad restrain himself any longer? What vow and what fear? He jumped up to the neighbour's porch and from there leapt onto the terrace. But hard-hearted Shirin had left the terrace

[1] Sounds like: 'Come.'

[2] Meow, which sounds like: 'Come, Sir'. *Mian* is the honorific term to address a man.

and gone downstairs. So he had to creep towards the courtyard. Quietly, he got onto the eaves, stretched out his neck and peeped down. What an interesting scene he saw! He put all four paws together, gathered his tail and laid it along his stomach crouched down and watched silently.

The clean little courtyard was lit with two electric bulbs. A third lamp burned at the head of the two bedsteads which were enclosed in white mosquito nets. Close to it, an electric fan (which Farhad hated vehemently) was making a *jhull jhull* sound as it gleamed and whirled. A little way away was a wooden divan covered with a white sheet. On this was spread a yellow carpet with pink flowers and a blue border. A bolster was placed on it. On one side of the bolster was a spittoon and on the other, a tin-coated copper betel box along with a small basket containing areca nuts. Next to the platform, on a stand, were two waterpots smelling of freshly wet earth: one a porous jug and the other a goblet, both with strings of jasmine flowers around their necks, also a small spouted water pitcher, and dishes for soap and lentil powder; all were new and glittering.

On the other side was a food cupboard (*nemat khana*)—its door open—and next to it, a small stove on which sat a pot of milk with a thick layer of cream on top.

Adjoining this courtyard was the smaller kitchen courtyard where there was a hen coop. From the kitchen came the smell of minced meat that had been boiled for *shami kababs* and from the hen coop came the sounds of the hens whispering. Farhad sat silently for a long time, and watched the scene. Finally, he was convinced that there were no humans in the house and if there were any in those small rooms made of cloth, surely they were asleep. He became audacious and started walking along the ledges towards the kitchen. Shirin, lying beside Iqbal's bride, had seen him. She used her paws to make an opening in the mosquito net, jumped off the bed and began to stroll around. When Farhad saw her, he abandoned the idea of a feast and turned his thoughts to much higher things. This was a strange passion indeed. Politely he called, *aaaooo*.

One of the white rooms moved and from it came a loud voice, 'Look, look! Your Farhad is here.'

From the second white room came a high, delicate voice, 'Don't say that. Never call him my Farhad. If he's a Farhad he must belong to that witch Shirin. Why would I need a Farhad?'

'So who's your Farhad?'

'I don't have one…ay …ay…except you…ay…'

'Come on, come on. Why did you stop?'

'Oh, let it be. I've just applied henna to my feet. Allah, it's barely been on a few moments. Will you please get up and close the food cupboard?'

The white room moved. It shivered and trembled and then seemed to rip. Farhad went past the courtyard and headed towards the lane while Iqbal Ahmad Sahib, the clean-shaven young Shift Engineer in the Electric Supply Company, wearing gold-framed spectacles and carrying the annual special issue of the magazine *Saqi*, emerged, wearing a black, striped nightsuit. When he was close to the food cupboard, his four-month-old wife called out in a strange tone that combined the conflicting qualities of delicacy, begging, pride, love and bashfulness, 'There's the minced meat that has been boiled for *kababs*. May you live long! Could you please bring that pot? And the milk—could you please put it in the food cupboard too.'

Without a word, Iqbal Ahmad slowly turned towards the kitchen and went in. He picked up the smoke-blackened pot with the tips of his fingers, carried it, holding it far from himself and put it in the cupboard. Then he put in the pot of milk and closed the cupboard. Just then the voice came again.

'Rahiman goes home early every evening. I can plead all I want but she never listens. God knows if she closed the hen coop. Please would you take a look at that too?'

Iqbal Ahmad mumbled as he walked from his bed towards the hen coop.

'Of all things, why keep a cat? This wretched creature of yours will invite all the tomcats of the city. Right now there's only one Farhad. Just wait—soon there will be dozens.'

Shirin, according to the traits of her race, had performed a bit of coquetry for the humpbacked cat belonging to the neighbourhood confectioner and had then crept back next to Iqbal's bride. The bride stroked her head with her henna-decorated hand and said, 'O you, Shirin! Do you have such wandering eyes?'

Shirin closed her eyes and making scratching noises, *khar khar*, pressed her head against the bride's hand, then squirmed and rubbed her body, right down to the tip of her tail.

Iqbal Ahmad, however, did not come back to his bed from the hen coop and instead went towards the hall. Startled, Nasima, the bride, asked: 'Where are you off to now? Oh, where are you going? Say something.'

'I am going to get some things to entertain Farhad.'

'O, for Allah's sake, don't! If you want me to live, I beg you, please don't do anything. You should never hit a cat. Have you not heard it said that if you ever hit a cat you should do so only with cotton wool? *Wah*, you are strange. The other day you hit the wretch with a wooden bat. I am superstitious. Oh what are you up to? What do you have in mind?'

'It's nothing. I'm arranging a feast for him. I'll feed Farhad Sahib some cream,' Iqbal Ahmad said as he disappeared into the room and brought out a small table, a large copper tray and a roll of wiring. He placed the tray on the table and put in it a china saucer containing cream and milk. Then he took one of the electric wires, exposed its end and placed it under the tray; the other wire he dipped into the milk in the saucer and then plugged the wires in.

'O Allah, Shirin! You've become a nuisance with your constant meowing. *Chayen mayen, chayen mayen*. O Rahiman! Ay Rahiman Bua, once you go into the storeroom you don't want to come out. Oh, come on out. Bring the ghee. *Bas bas*, that's enough. I only need to fry two more pieces. Hurry up, they're getting burnt. Eidu, my brother, will you wash that?'

The biting cold evenings turn rapidly into night. Her husband had told her the party would be at five o'clock. Nasima had prepared all kinds of savouries and sweets. She was frying the last slices of baked bread and thinking how delighted her husband would be when he saw all of this, when she heard the sound of the bicycle bell. 'I'm coming *Miyan*.' Rahiman called as she ran. With the edge of her *dupatta*, Nasima wiped off the ash from the fire that had settled on her face. Mr Iqbal Ahmad, wearing patterned woollen socks, khaki shorts, a blue blazer with a six-inch long and three-inch wide bow tie round his neck, and a dandyish flat cap with a fawn-colored feather in it, entered the house. He put the package he was carrying on the divan, pulled at the strings and tore open the paper wrapping. Four tins emerged. There was a tin of butter, a can of raspberry jam, a tin of cheese and a tin of 555 cigarettes. He took out the penknife from his pocket and got busy opening them. When the most stubborn of them all, the tin of butter, which put up a great deal of resistance, was open, he called out to his wife.

'What's the matter? Will you come out or not? It looks like nothing is ready yet. I knew it!'

'Not at all. It's all done. Everything's ready. I'll be there in a moment,' Nasima said as she emerged from the kitchen, dragging a broken slipper on her foot.

'What are you saving the new slippers for? Anyway, forget it. It's useless saying anything to you. Go, bring me a loaf of bread and I'll make sandwiches. Everywhere else wives do this kind of work but here I have to do it. My wife can't do a thing. What can I say? I got delayed because I had to buy all this stuff in Aminabad. Come on, bring it. Why are you just standing there listening to me? Bring the loaf of bread; the eggs and the stove too.'

On Nasima's face was dejection, panic and fear. In a soft voice she asked. '*Naan pao. Naan pao*?'[3]

'Yes, yes, I mean *naan pao*. Why don't you call it a double-roti? Alas! Those who used to make *naan pao* and those who used to eat it are all dead. But my wife insists on calling a loaf of bread *naan pao*. She can't say "racket"—she calls it a bat! All right, forget the loaf of bread, where is the *naan pao*?'

'I made a mistake.'

'O, that's nothing new! What is it now?'

'I must have taken leave of my senses.'

'*Arey*, what is it? Out with it.'

'You can say what you want. Without any doubt, I've made a mistake. You did say something about this yesterday but God knows how I misunderstood. I have used the *naan pao*...eh...loaf of bread to make dessert.'

Iqbal Ahmad's elbow came to rest on the wooden platform and his head on the palm of his hand. In a feeble voice, he asked, 'And the eggs?'

[3] Old-fashioned term for baked bread weighing half a pound.

Some life crept back into Nasima. In a louder, more confident voice she said. 'They are ready. I have already fried them.'

'O Lord, help me! That's the end of the omelet. O, my fate!'

Nasima's face lost colour. Her eyes brimmed with tears as she stood there listening to him.

'Oh, I knew something like this would happen. Everyone can have a party but not me. What could I do? They all insisted that I throw a party to celebrate my promotion to Assistant Engineer. The other day Robertson had a party and what a…let it be! Maqbul threw a party and what a competent wife he has! Even the cakes were baked at home. The cakes I brought—are they still here? Or have you done something to them too?'

Nasima brought the cakes and gave them to him. Meekly, she summoned Eidu. She arranged all that she had prepared in plates. Iqbal Ahmad, while scolding and shouting at Eidu, laid out all the stuff on a table in the front room. Then he explained everything to Eidu—how to serve the tea, where to stand, how to place and remove the dishes. The lad was Indian and was going to serve Indian food; a poor man can harass only another poor man. Laughing and joking, the four friends who had been invited arrived on their bicycles.

Thank God, the party was successful in every way. Robertson loved the yoghurt dumplings and said, 'How wonderful it would be if my wife learnt to cook like this. Will your wife teach her?'

Maqbul was more straightforward, 'Friend, you did well to get all these things prepared. Allah be praised, everything is delicious.'

No one touched the cakes. Iqbal Ahmad was very happy. Things had eventually turned out well. Eidu, the new servant, was completely crude but even he stayed silent and did not display much of his uncouthness. It is true that a couple of times, for no reason, he tried to join the laughter but he covered his teeth the moment Iqbal Ahmad stared at him.

The party was conducted graciously and tastefully, but just at the moment when they were about to leave the table, God help them, a calamity suddenly descended from the sky, hissing and jumping. The table toppled, dishes were broken and the guests ran, crashed into each other, got entangled among the chairs and fell down.

Since three in the afternoon, whenever he got a chance, Eidu had been stealing things and hiding them in a copper lentil-powder pot, so that he could enjoy them at leisure at night. The pot, covered with a leaf, was kept close to the skylight. The ill-fated Farhad, in search of Shirin, chanced upon it. How could he not smell the food and since the smell was of fried delicacies, how could he ignore it? But the pot had a narrow opening and even though his head slipped in, it was difficult for him to get it out. He turned into a blinded buffalo. He writhed and wriggled, and eventually fell through the skylight. And when he heard strange sounds from the humans, he put out all his claws, hissed and began to spring from ground to sky and sky to ground. The wretch leapt two yards high each time!

It was dark all around. A pall of light smoke had spread slowly across the rooftops. The sun was setting on the western horizon. Just a few black-tinged clouds lurked in the sky. A light buzz could be heard from the bazaar. From a nearby house came the faint sound of an infant crying, and holding not only his breath but the same note. Darkness had seeped into the depths of the environs and into the roots of the walls. On a wall that was covered in effloresced salt, sat Shirin, miserable, staring at the parapet in front of her. She seemed lost in deeply melancholic thoughts. What did the poor thing know of memories and their associations, tragedies and their causes or the lessons that could be drawn from them? Whenever she saw her friend Nasima sad or in pain, a life-crushing sorrow would overcome her too. The reasons why Nasima was in physical agony or emotional grief did not matter to her. Neither did she remember the two earlier occasions when Nasima had delivered premature babies. This was the third such child and he too died soon after he was born, almost taking Nasima with him.

The first time Nasima had gone to her natal home before she went into labour. Along with her mother, her aunts and brother were in attendance. The next time she could not go home even though her mother was still alive. She had vowed never to go to her brother's home again. But when the time came she went running over holding her stomach. Who was going to help her this third time? Her mother was dead. Her aunt refused to come. Her brother's wife was in the last stages of her own pregnancy. Nasima's in-laws were upstarts, crazy in their quest for recognition and prominence. The moment they moved a yard up, they became arrogant and lost sight of the world below them.

Iqbal Ahmad was of their flesh and blood and acted exactly in the same way, knocking down the step below him the moment he reached the step above. When from Shift Engineer he became Assistant Engineer, he divorced his friends and made new, better ones. When he was promoted to Resident Engineer, he stopped meeting these friends too. He showed great politeness to others. He abandoned simplicity, displayed amazing concern and affection, and then, with what beautiful precision, abandoned them too! Who came this time when his wife fell ill? Lipstick-wearing birds like Mrs Jha, Mrs Rahman, Miss Farhat! They came carrying cameras, novels and parasols, debating fascism and socialism, chattering and laughing. They drank tea, ate chocolates, smoked cigarettes, sat for twenty to thirty minutes, expressed sympathy, gave advice, turned into physicians and then left. Before leaving, they again gave sympathetic advice.

'Mr Iqbal, you must hire a nurse for a week or two. What do these midwives know about nursing? And the patient must stay in her bed and should not even be allowed to sit up. She must get rest, complete rest. No noise or disturbance. You too must go into her room as infrequently as possible. In fact you shouldn't go in at all. She needs solitude and rest, that's all. And…this house…it isn't good enough. Why don't you buy a small house in the suburbs? You can buy them cheap.'

The result of this was that the very next day, Mrs Heel, a certified nurse who was to be paid four rupees in ready cash every day and who had gotten her name from her third husband, was imposed on Nasima. And it was she, this amazing, hope-giving healer who with her endless efforts and constant attention very soon pulled Nasima away from the edge of the grave, and saved her from the claws of certain death and left her to live a long, dead life.

She did not know when in the dark room she regained consciousness. Her benumbed heart was trembling. Her hands shook and she felt dizzy. Was *Amma*, her mother, here or not? She had no control over her memory. She opened her eyes and saw someone moving. Who is it? Who is this? Mrs Heel turned around and found the lady conscious. 'O Khuda, thank you, O Lord! Begum, you are all right now. Don't worry. You'll be well soon.'

Nasima felt another movement. She opened her eyes and her vision had improved. She could see everything clearly. Her mind stopped. Recollections and memories created a commotion. Her mind guided her again. House…home…woman…a *mem*, actually a lady doctor…he next to her…man…my man…they…they…

they...Allah, thanks, thanks to you…they, they, what are they doing? …he is staring at the doctor. And he is staring at her in that way! The doctor is beautiful. They, yes, he is staring at her with that look. He still hasn't looked this way towards me. His voice! 'Mrs Heel….' English…English….

The voice of the *mem*! English…English. 'Mrs Iqbal….' English… English.

'I should close my eyes and listen.'

She closed them and the voices faded, while shouts of 'the palanquin is here…the palanquin has come…' grew louder. 'The palanquin is here, welcome it,' echoed from every direction and scores of palanquins began to encircle Nasima.[4]

Slowly, Farhad's head appeared above the dark wall, then his chest, and then his legs. Now Farhad walked along the walls towards Shirin. It was fairly dark. In the entire sky there was only a fleck of red left. The child was still crying. Far away a drum began to play. A few house-bats were bounding around in the air. Saying '*aao, aao,*' Farhad came near her. In Shirin's wild eyes shone two tears. From the wall she jumped on to the roof and then quickly disappeared downstairs.

'I devote myself to you! I sacrifice myself to your blessed eyes, Shirin. I would sacrifice the world's pearls for those two tears.'

These days Shirin was often depressed and sad, and Farhad was severely affected by this. The poor cat did everything he could to dispel Shirin's gloom. He would come to Shirin, carrying a rat from the street, a squirrel from the walls or a small parakeet that he had grabbed from some faraway home, and would sometimes

[4] The palanquin is associated, among other things, with a bride. Welcoming of the bride is one of the most joyous rituals of a wedding.

succeed in getting her to play with these half-dead creatures. But after a while Shirin would again grow dispirited. He had to take great risks as he continued these unsuccessful attempts to distract her. To spite Iqbal Ahmad he would come every day and was now not afraid of ordinary weapons like shoes and paper weights. All he wanted was to allay Shirin's sorrow. Often, he could not find her and would enter the rooms to look for her, but he could not fight his nature the day he smelled cheese in the open food cupboard. He postponed his search for Shirin and went towards it. The moment he entered, the door of the cupboard slammed shut behind him. Farhad jumped with all his might. He banged his head against the top and at this very moment Iqbal Ahmad reached the cupboard with a thin rope in his hand. Farhad hissed, raised the hair on his back, drew out his claws and slashed at the meshing of the food cupboard. He could have torn apart this hard wire mesh but he did not get the time. First he began to be caned from every side. Then a rug was folded and thrown over the cupboard. When the door opened and he jumped out, he got entangled in the rug. God have mercy, what a plight he was in! He was squeezed from above and wrapped up so tightly that he began to suffocate. Because of the pressure from all around, he felt as if his bones would break. He was unable to use his claws. He was rolled around. Then his tail was pulled out and on it a thin rope was tied so tightly that he was in excruciating pain. He stayed in this extremely unpleasant situation for a long time. Mercifully he was released but he now found himself in the narrow confines of a tin box. The middle of his tail hurt so much that it felt as if his tail might have been severed at that point. The poor cat could not even turn his face towards his tail because he had no space to move. In these tight dark confines, there was neither air nor light. This was the first time in his life he had had to deal with such darkness. His claws were of no use because they slipped off the tin when they scraped it.

In pain and anger Farhad began to shout *'na aoon, na aoon,'*[5] but this had no effect. He stayed thus for hours, not knowing what was happening to him. Some times his steel prison would shake and then become still. Sometimes when it shook, it continued to shake. He had reached a stage where, because of lack of oxygen he lay indifferent in a half-faint. His voice grew faint. It was in this state that he felt some fresh air. He took a long breath and life crept back into him. Then he detected light and more fresh air. There was a clatter; someone was opening the box. He was prepared for whatever struggle lay ahead. The box opened with a clang. Suddenly, there was light. *Fash shoon*! Farhad leapt out with great force. '*Aai*, my Jesus Christ!' Mrs Heel screamed as she fell back on the sofa and Farhad, flaying twenty claws in the air, landed in her lap. Since neither of them had any attachment to the other, they separated as fast as they had united. Memsahib ran to the bathroom and Farhad towards the verandah. She found peace once she had locked the bathroom door but there was a clanging, rattling curse now chasing Farhad. It would not leave him. He ran as fast as he could but that rattling nuisance followed him.

Exhausted from the running, Farhad reached Hazratganj Crossing. There, two dozen, fair, dark and hunch-backed *baba log*[6] were up to all sorts of mischief. They attacked Farhad from every direction. One kicked him, another hit him with a hockey stick. One two-and-a-half-feet-high beetroot lookalike turned out to be like Hitler. He threw a lasso at Farhad which landed on his tail and immediately formed a knot that forced Farhad to tug and run away,

[5] Sounds like: 'I won't come.'

[6] Could include British, Anglo-Indian, Eurasian or upper middle class anglicized Indian kids.

leaving half his tail behind. Anyway, with the tail went his sorrow and he managed to save his life. Also, with the tail stayed behind the rattle that had been tied to his tail with a copper wire and had followed him like a ghost, scaring the life out of him. Now, free of his tail and its attendant nuisance and feeling lighter, he ran straight towards home. Where was the need to go along roads, streets, lanes and neighbourhoods? He did not have to ask for directions. Nature has bestowed a special instinct on cats so that no matter where you lock them or how far away you take them, they head straight for home when released. Farhad too—with his docked tail—crossed roofs, drains, streets, avoided dogs, scared the life out of hens, pigeons and mice, suffered blows and with the stump of his tail like a fountain pen dripping red ink the whole way, finally reached home.

Life does not stand still. Shirin and Farhad's life had now taken a new turn. Love, with all its joyful quests and disappointments, anxieties and vexations, its wonderful involvements, had ended. Now they led a simple, dull life with Nasima. Farhad, completely indifferent to the confectioner's shop, spent all his time here. There were no longer any threats to him in this house because Iqbal Ahmad had completely stopped coming here. Having converted his new wife from Mrs Heel to Mrs Iqbal, he was now living in Hazratganj.

The defeated, helpless Nasima lived her life, indifferent not only to the meek and despondent Shirin and her Farhad, but also to her own household, her clothes, money, even her own life, and remained continually in a daze and stupor. Even though Iqbal still gave her fifty rupees a month to run the house, she did not care if she had money or not. Rahiman and Eidu, who did care about money, had established their control over the kitchen and the store. Shirin and Farhad seemed to control the rest of the languishing household. These two were all over the rooms, stores and verandah. There was dust and dirt everywhere. Scraps of paper and cloth rags were scattered all around. Spiky grass, which stuck to clothes, had sprouted at various places in the courtyard. Tufts of a wild herb grew on and around the hen coop. Near the entrance, a large spittoon had been lying on its side for so long that it was almost covered by another herb. Also close to the entrance, saplings had sprung from the pits of mangoes that Eidu had eaten. Nasima's own cot had stood so long in the same place in a corner of the verandah that it had made a dark rectangular mark on the floor.

Nasima spent all her time either splitting areca nuts for betel or reading *Raah-e Najaat* or *Halima Dai*.[7] Not only were these the only two books she had, but she was not capable of reading any others. She had read these books so often that she knew them by heart. In each couplet of the short and simple poems of *Halima Dai* she found amazing revelations and undisclosed pain. Even though she did not know what all the words meant, she believed that this sacred book was full of bodings for a future peaceful and happy life. She used to read it with such pure emotion and faith that her tears would not stop as long as the book was in front of her. Since the mistress was crying, Rahiman considered it her duty to accompany her either with occasional tears or at least with constant sniffling, wiping the discharge from her nose on the legs of the cot.

One afternoon, Nasima was reading the tale of Halima Dai. As usual, Rahiman was sitting beside her on the floor, on her haunches, holding the frame of the cot and listening. Nasima held down the pages of the book that had cost two *paise* and pressed them against

[7] Dai Halima was the Prophet's wet nurse. Verse narratives based on religious *qissa* (stories) were very popular.

a pillow with both hands. Rocking back and forth,[8] she read out each couplet twice or three times in a simple, sombre tone and wiped her tears with her *dupatta*, when suddenly a panting Eidu, abandoning his kite on the terrace, came running down and said, 'Begum Sahiba, someone has come.'

As he finished saying this, someone rattled the latch on the door. Nasima raised her voice and called, 'Who is it? Why don't you say who you are?'

'Mistress, who knows who it is!'

'O Rahiman! Go and see. Ask who it is.'

From the entrance, a tense, worried voice called out. 'Iqbal Ahmad, Iqbal Ahmad.'

Signs of happiness and anxiety appeared on Nasima's face. Quickly, she rearranged her *dupatta,* saying, 'O Rahiman, go and see. It's Respected Brother (Miyan Bhai).' She hurriedly got off her cot, put on her slippers, went forward a few steps and stood respectfully. Rahiman, after taking her time rearranging her own *dupatta*, stopped her giggling and making of a hundred useless gestures, and peeped into the portico. The she drew back, contracted and contorted herself, and in syrupy tones murmured, 'Come, sir, come inside.'

Tall, dressed in white, with a sparse black beard on a wide face, a wheatish complexion tinged with red, a stick in one hand and a leather hand bag in the other, Nasima's brother Munshi Kazim Hussain, Sub-registrar, entered the house in a hurry, then stopped and stood still in the middle of the courtyard. Nasima was forced to bow and greet him for the third time. Her brother, in a loud voice, first proclaimed his faith 'There is no God but Allah and Muhammad is his Prophet.'

[8] A motion usually associated with the reading/memorizing of the Quran.

Nasima panicked. Abandoning her bashfulness and manners, she moved forward. 'Is everything all right, Respected Brother? O my Allah, is everything all right? What is the matter, Respected Brother?'

Munshi Kazim Hussain, his eyes fixed on Nasima, bent his knees as he stood, slowly lowered himself and gently placed his stick and hand bag on the ground; with his eyes still on Nasima, he raised himself until he was standing erect again. He raised both his hands and beginning with his forehead and eyes, stroked his face up to the tip of his beard and then in a Quran-reading tone said, 'May Allah be praised.'

Except for Shirin and Farhad, the scene was frightening for everyone else. Farhad, followed by Shirin, left the house, climbed the stairs, went to the terrace and did not return for quite a few hours.

During this period there was a lot of talking and listening between brother and sister and the atmosphere became peaceful again. Kazim told his sister that he had received a telegram from Iqbal Ahmad, saying that if he wanted to see his sister alive he should come immediately because she was ill and would live only for a very short time.

Nasima now told him her story and admitted that in her letters she had not been telling him the truth about her situation. She also admitted that she had received his letters asking her to come to him and that she had not answered them. She was sobbing incessantly and in between hiccoughs, she said, 'Respected Brother, I pray that you live for a thousand years, prosper, see much happiness and bring home daughters-in-law. This is what I pray for. But please try and understand that this is my home. How can I leave it while I'm still alive? I want to die within the threshold of this house. This is what I really want. I can't change fate. I'll shame myself both in this world and the next if I leave this home. This is my home. How can I leave it?'

With great care and after checking everything out, Shirin and Farhad did return home but they kept a suspicious eye both on the sleeping Kazim Hussain—who had not slept the previous night—and on his stick. The moment he awoke in the morning, they left the house and began to wander on the roof tops. Farhad found a squirrel nest hidden in the staircase beams of the neighbouring double-storeyed house. This led to very pleasurable exercise. Shirin and Farhad both got busy trying to scale the wall of *lakhori*[9] bricks to get to the nest. Even though there was no possibility of their reaching the nest, they had fun climbing and falling off the wall because the mother squirrel, sitting on a cornice in the wall, had fluffed up the fur on her tail and was making a continuous din of *chirr chir chir chirr*. They enjoyed scaring her.

In the midst of all this, Shirin heard very loud, crackling and argumentative sounds coming from her house. She began to worry. She thought of Nasima and immediately headed home. Iqbal Ahmad and Kazim Hussain were standing in the courtyard, verbally assaulting each other at the top of their voices. Nasima stood holding the pillar of the kitchen and sobbing. Rahiman sat on the floor on her haunches, her face resting on Nasima's calf, and wept. To flatter her mistress, she had been crying along with her for two months, nay, for two years, over Dai Halima's tale. She had for months, nay years, been claiming two annas a seer for salt that she perhaps bought for half that price. But those were professional, not personal matters. Today, putting those concerns aside, she was loudly crying her heart out. Her heart sank at the thought of being separated from the innocent Nasima, who was innately so pure and honest.

[9] A kind of small, slim brick from the Mughal period.

Eidu stood next to the water pitcher rack and kept crying as he drank cup after cup of water. He had forgotten his love of kites and tops in his distress at the thought of being separated from the honest, dear and kind person who loved him more than a mother would. He wished he could be transformed into the cloth cover for her books and go away with her forever. Every time he thought about it, a spasm of weeping would overcome him and he would drink more water. Shirin wished she could chew up the wind-pipes of Iqbal Ahmad and Kazim Hussain. She did not care what they were saying to each other but she found their screaming at each other very unpleasant. She loitered around Nasima's legs, saying *maoon, maoon*.

The sobbing, the hiccoughs and the *maoon maaons* were of no use and Nasima's little flower-garden from which spring had departed as soon as it arrived and which had lain abandoned for years, ceased to exist. They had to leave. The end. The end.

Some stuff was moved from here to there. Some went out from inside and some from outside came in. Some earthen water-pots were smashed. Some papers were shredded. Some old, worn-out clothes were torn. Some were given away and some thrown away. Shards of broken china and tins were thrown here and there. The garbage in the house first doubled and then trebled. This meant that Nasima's belongings had been sorted and packed. A covered cart rumbled up. The luggage was loaded on it. Nasima turned and looked at the house where she had been imprisoned for seven years. She broke down and cried again. What could Shirin do? She cried *maoon maoon* and wished she could sacrifice herself for Nasima's happiness.

Kazim Hussain barked. 'That's enough! Haven't you cried enough already? For God's sake get up.'

Nasima lifted up Shirin, left the house and followed her brother into the horse carriage. Animals do not complain if you forget them or ignore them. But if you give them love and attention they are happy and grateful. Today, Nasima had taken Shirin into her arms after a year. She was happy beyond measure. Even though she was very scared of the rattling, shaking and jerking carriage, she sat clinging to Nasima. The carriage reached the third class waiting room at the railway station. The luggage was unloaded. They got off. Countless people swarmed around. Among them were innumerable fierce dogs. Shirin was suffocating inside Nasima's *burqa* but was very scared when she looked out and saw the crowd.

She had been highly agitated since she arrived here. She did not know what to do, where to go or where to hide. She slipped from Nasima's arms and then, bewildered, tried to follow her. Two dogs pounced on her and the poor thing ran, and ran in a way that would never again allow her to find Nasima. It is an animal's instinct to return home. Her small brain told her to return to the same house where she would find her lady, so she headed straight for home.

It was two in the afternoon when she reached home. A few kites were gliding in the sky. Small whirlwinds descended from roof to courtyard and blew in corners. Scraps of paper and twigs from the broom jumped around in circles, moved upwards towards the terrace and then dropped dead in despair and grief. Rubbish lay everywhere. The vessel containing coal lay broken in front of the kitchen. Coal and ashes were scattered all over. In the verandah, Nasima's old cot stood on two legs, leaning against a wall, far from its old place. It seemed immersed in grief, its arms stretched upwards in prayer. Nearby, Rahiman's tin betel box lay on its face, weeping. In silence. Away from the world, living the life of transients, three people had been passing their life in this deserted house, on their own, quietly. They were no burden to the world.

Nor did they disturb the world in any way. But today they were no longer there. There was a lock on the main door. Shirin and Farhad would roam around for hours calling out *maoon maoon* but with no results. Evening came and darkness began to spread but there was no one to light a lamp in this house.

Shirin and Farhad hated the sight of Iqbal Ahmad more than any other. Both viewed him with disgust and contempt. Whatever had happened in the past and although he was no old friend of theirs, this was after all his house. What right did he have to act like a tyrant, create chaos and throw things around? The two decided that come what may, they would not leave this house. They sat hidden amongst the stuff in a room until Iqbal Ahmad came close to them. They would then run to another room and hide there. For two hours at a stretch, Iqbal Ahmad, drenched in sweat, with a cigar in his mouth, went around dragging tables and chairs, pushing beds and rattling utensils. He then locked the rooms and left the house. He locked the main door, got into his Baby Austin and drove away, raising dust. This happened the day after Nasima had gone, and Shirin and Farhad, like lover and beloved, were left in the room to die together.

For a while they did not understand the significance of their being locked in. Once the house was quiet, they began to play games. The more randomly the stuff was piled up, the more interested they were in it because they could hear mice rustling about inside it or occasionally see a head peeping out. After a great deal of effort, Farhad even managed to catch a mouse and when he brought the half dead creature to the bed, Shirin, who had been sitting on a chair placed on a table next to the bed, jumped and snatched it away. For some time they played at snatching the dead mouse from each other. However, it was getting to be evening. The room became dark. In these last days of the monsoon heat the humid air in the room felt suffocating. Leaving the dead mouse, they both came to the door. They paced in front of it, scratched it, went around the room and then came back to the door. The room had only this one door. Looking for another was useless. Yet they went round the room all night, looking for another exit, and on each round, they stopped to rub their noses into the cracks of the door. In the room there was nothing for them to eat. However, there was a copper pot filled with water and they would sip from it as they continued their futile, endless search for another day.

Cats hunt mice only for fun. They chew their heads and discard them. Their religion does not allow them to eat the flesh of mice. Now they were so hungry that they both relished the mouse they had killed the day before. When nourishment reached their stomachs and when, in their hunger, they realized how delicious mice were, they began to look for mice. Sadly, because of their continuous presence for thirty-two hours, all the mice had left, cursing the room and the cats.

They stayed hungry for four days and four nights. Now the two searched nooks and crannies and ate crickets. After all, can only water sustain you? As time passed they weakened. The two sat at the door and mechanically made sounds of *maoon* and *aoon*.

With their wandering minds and dim eyesight they saw mice peeping out of every corner. They would rise on the strength of hope and stagger back to the door, crying '*maoon maoon,* in dying tones. As more time passed, their limbs and senses gave way. Their voices too sounded feeble and came only after long intervals.

Ten days passed. Shirin, who lay at some distance from Farhad, fell silent. Every half an hour or so, Farhad would utter a feeble *'aaaaaam'*. His vision had faded but his eyes would sometimes spontaneously brighten up. They would look all around for food and then darkness would descend again. During one of these dying flickers he looked around and saw a small heap of meat lying nearby. He pushed with his hind legs and with the help of his front claws slowly moved towards it. What did he find there? A deception! It wasn't meat but the dried-up skeletal remains of his beloved Shirin who was still breathing weakly. Yes, it was Shirin, the same Shirin. He looked at her, smelt her, then turned around and dragged his dead weight back with his claws, inch by inch, to the door and collapsed. It took hours for each hour to pass.

A gush of life passed through him again. His blood surged a bit. A sense of sight returned to his eyes and again he was deceived by the lump of flesh. Farhad dragged himself to it but it wasn't meat but his own Shirin. He smelt her. There was a smell. It was the scent of Shirin. And with Shirin's scent was mixed the smell of meat. He wanted to move away from there but he was too weak. He lost control over his head which hit the floor and he fainted. When he opened his eyes again, he could smell meat. He saw that Shirin's gaunt frame was still alive. Suddenly Farhad's incomplete, bestial mind merged Shirin and food into one thought. An inch at a time, he moved his head, opened his jaws and squeezed Shirin's throat. She opened her eyes slowly, looked at Farhad and for the last time uttered a low *'maoon'*. Farhad used all his strength to press his sharp teeth into Shirin's windpipe and then lay still. He had no more strength left. Slowly, a few drops of drying blood trickled onto his tongue. Two drops at a time it went down his throat and slowly some life returned to Farhad's limbs. Now he ate some meat. He felt stronger. He also felt thirsty. He went to the pot and drank some water. His eyes opened. His limbs came alive again. The real, gnawing hunger was reborn. Now he bent over Shirin as if she was a normal meal. In a little while no signs of her remained except for a few bones.

After prolonged starvation, the intoxicated Farhad, with his stomach full, sat on a trunk and began to doze. He had not been sitting for long when there were sounds outside. He heard the voices of Iqbal Ahmad and his servants. The latch rattled. Exhausted, intoxicated, weak, his stomach bloated, Farhad got up, unsteadily walked out of the room and went up the stairs to the terrace.

For a long time after the incident, people saw an ugly, black, dock-tailed tomcat uttering fierce sounds as it walked along the walls. Deprived of both intellect and memory, Farhad searched for Shirin on roofs, and in lanes and houses.

Farhad! O wild Farhad, victim of unheard-of cruelty, your being is a being worthy of praise. No matter how many unpleasant aspects there were to Shirin's death, we must remember that it came instantly and its impact ended almost immediately. But you, O Nasima! When will death come to you? When will your woes end? How long will you continue to live in your brother's house, cooking bread, scrubbing utensils? How long will you continue to be the punching bag for your spoilt and badly behaved nephews and nieces?

The Voiceless

When they heard of the five hundred rupee prize, they all queued up to take turns. An Indian rider, a Pathan from Kabul, a white man from the armoury, a soldier and countless others entered the circus ring, one by one, to ride the mare. They made every attempt but let alone getting astride the mare, they were not even able to touch the reins of her bridle. Whenever someone entered the ring, she would pull back her ears, bare her teeth, neigh and attack; and he would turn around, stumble and fall as he ran out of the circus enclosure. When a few stubborn ones, waving a cane or a whip, managed to stay on, the mare would whirl and kick so wildly that they too would be forced to leave, ashamed and embarrassed.

The circus manager, standing on the small wall encircling the ring, turned around, looked at the spectators and announced again, 'There are so many gentlemen, soldiers and lads here. Will someone else try? Come on! Is anyone brave enough? I'll give a prize of five hundred rupees to anyone who can get on the mare and ride four paces.'

Thousands of people were packed into the circus on couches, chairs and on stands rising to the roof. But no one else seemed to have the guts to volunteer. People sat, quiet, embarrassed; in front of them, in the small show ring, the gleaming black, smooth, lean, healthy, young, agile and lively mare, arched her neck, neighed, flicked her tail and shook her head as she stamped the ground with her front hooves. Each move radiated the pride of victory, the arrogance of beauty and the vibrancy of youth. While all eyes were fixed on her, the secret door to the ring gently opened and a girl entered like a breeze, her whip swishing like lightning. The mare jumped, frisked and began to run. The whip swished again and then again. The mare was running around the ring with all her might. All eyes were now fixed on the white human-calf. Short, plump, with black hair and her circus costume clinging to her, she was stunning. Her hand, her leg, her bust, her neck, her head, her eyes, each attracted attention because each embodied youth. Each of her moves was playful and mischievous. Her hands fluttered, her feet danced and there was a spring in her neck. The world stared at her but she was indifferent. Whirling the whip, she effortlessly leapt onto the galloping mare. With both hands she tidied her flowing hair. Then, she stood up on the running mare's bare back, and the mare began to run faster around the circle. Half her hair escaped its pink ribbon and flew behind her. Her rounded legs, in skin-tight pyjamas, quivered. She waved her arms in the air and danced the ballet on the galloping mare's back. Everyone's eyes were fixed on her but the hidden door had silently opened again; the mare turned towards it and disappeared along with her rider. For a few seconds there was stunned silence. The applause that followed brought the house down.

Within a few days of the circus' arrival in Lucknow, the mare and the girl's fame began to spread. All sorts of tales circulated about their beauty, magnificence, liveliness and the girl's riding skills. Gossip kept spreading. Some believed that the girl was of loose morals. Others would point to the significance of the circus manager keeping such a strict watch on her that no one could ever meet or see her. There were those who suspected that she had a liaison with the owner of the circus. Others were convinced that she was actually his daughter. However, all these were fabrications because no one ever got to know or meet any of those who worked in the circus. High canvas screens surrounded the animals' cages and staff tents, hiding them from the public gaze. The manager had firmly instructed everyone in the circus not to meet anyone or leave the encampment. In these circumstances, a certain section of Lucknow's populace which included pleasure-seekers, vagabonds and impoverished aristocrats, began to spend time loitering around the enclosure. One would try to peep under the screens and another through the door. Anyone who caught so much as a glimpse of an elephant's leg, a tiger's cage or an employee, would go around retailing long eyewitness accounts of what he had seen.

This gossip ended up reaching the ears of Mahmud Ali Khan, *taluqadar* of Daliyabad, who turned up one day to watch the show. Special seating arrangements had been made for him. He watched all the acts with amazement and liked them all. However, he liked the one with the girl and the mare the most. When the show ended, he summoned the manager. He lavished praise on the show, particularly on the girl and the mare. He even tried to meet the girl, saying that he wanted to reward her. However, when the manager told him that was impossible because the girl only came out for her performance, he departed, gifting his wrist watch to the manager and leaving fifty rupees for the girl.

He turned up again the next day to watch a show. In fact, he arrived very early. He again called for the manager and talked to him for a long time about various things, making sure to bring back the conversation to the girl and the mare. The manager did not have much time to spend with the Nawab Sahib because he had to get the show going. After the show he returned without being summoned. The Nawab Sahib gave him five hundred rupees as a token of appreciation. They talked for a long time and it was late when the Nawab Sahib left. He invited the manager to his palace for a meal the next day. The manager knew very well why the Nawab Sahib was being so generous and attentive.

Every one knew of the sixty-five-year-old Nawab, his hundred-year-old palace and his wealth. The worldly-wise circus manager knew it was an opportunity and decided to make as much money as he could. He acted after a great deal of thought and with foresight. After the meal, when the matter of the girl came up, the manager turned very nervous and anxious. He did not want to talk about her at all. He said her father and brother were with her and kept a strict watch on her. Nothing could be done about her. However, after enough blandishments, and much initial stammering, he suggested the following plan:

'Nawab Sahib, I will do this only because of the tremendous hospitality and generosity you have shown. Sir, I hope you realize what a dangerous task I am undertaking. If anything goes wrong, I will spend ten to twelve years in jail doing hard labour. Anyway, no matter what, I'll see that you get what you want. Tomorrow we are performing our last show and will leave for Kanpur the next day. On Monday morning, drive your car yourself, come to the entrance and wait. The girl hasn't been keeping too well. I will fool her by saying that the car has come to take her to a doctor and will bring her and put her in the car. She'll never suspect what is happening. Let her sit in the car, then drive her away. Don't speak to her. Make whatever arrangements you need to make. As for me, her father and brother will chop me to bits. I cannot even imagine the troubles that will follow. I will have to report the matter to the police or else, I will be in more serious trouble. I'll also have to buy her father and brother's silence and therefore want to make it clear to you, Sir, that I will not be able to do this for less than ten thousand rupees. God alone knows if any of it will be left for me. After I pay off her relatives and the police, if there is anything left for me, good. Otherwise, I'll be doing hard labour in jail for nothing. Nawab Sahib, I request you again. Forget about the girl. You won't be able to manage her.'

The circus had been at Lal Bagh for twenty days. They performed their last show on Sunday and began preparing to leave on Monday morning. The grooms rode off on the horses early in the morning. The other animals' cages were being loaded onto carts. The tents were being taken down and folded; everyone was busy. On one side sat an elephant on whom a lot of baggage with a few monkeys tied to it was loaded. The other elephants stood around, swaying. The manager's tent was still up and he sat on an armchair in front of it, waiting for the Nawab Sahib. Various men would come to him and he would issue instructions, look at his watch and sit back to wait.

Close to nine o'clock the horn of Nawab Sahib's car sounded. The Nawab Sahib, wearing a *kurta* and *pajama*, was himself driving a large car with curtained windows. The manager walked up to him and greeted him. The Nawab Sahib's eyes were gleaming. His face was flushed with nervousness. He smiled and in a worried tone asked, 'How are things?'

The manager answered in a relaxed tone, 'Everything is in place.'

Nawab Sahib quickly reacted, 'That's good. Go and get her.'

Still in a calm tone, the manager, said: 'You needn't worry about my end of things. What about yours? Look, Nawab Sahib, it will be impossible for me to come to your palace again after this incident. Nor should any of your men come to me. I don't want to involve anyone else in this.'

The Nawab Sahib quickly pulled out a wrapped-up bundle of notes from under the seat. He unwrapped and re-wrapped the bundle as he said, 'The money is here, don't worry. Get the girl into the car and you can have the money. Go, hurry up! It doesn't look proper for me to be seen waiting here.'

The manager looked at the bank notes once again. He walked away, smiling, and entered the screened enclosure. He went to his own tent, peeped in and gestured with his hand. The girl, wearing the same tight performing costume, walked out smiling and followed the manager. Outside, the engine of the car was already running. The Nawab Sahib sat ready, holding the steering wheel with both hands. As soon as the two came near, the Nawab Sahib looked greedily at the girl. Her cheeks were red and her lips painted. A ribbon was tied across her forehead. Below, her hair flowed loose on to her shoulders. She glanced at the Nawab Sahib and with a smile walked up to the car. The manager opened the door and she got in. The manager shut the door and approached Nawab Sahib who gave him the bundle of notes and started the car. In a moment the car rounded the corner and disappeared from sight. Outside the screened enclosure, the manager stood on the footpath, looking at the bundle of money with a smile; then he stuffed it into his pocket and went inside.

The car moved noisily, taking many tu[illegible] as it went through various neighbourhoods till it reached the edge of the city. From here it headed towards Daliyabad where all arrangements had been carefully made, under strict orders. The moment the car turned into the gate leading to the female wing of the palace, the large main gate was closed. Inside this large gate was a courtyard with a few flower beds, trees and bushes. Here sat a few employees. The car stopped in front of a high plinth which led to a large hall. A fat, middle-aged maid, wearing heaps of silver jewellery, came to the car and opened the door. Pompously, she said, 'Please alight and come with me.' The girl, still silent, still smiling and still happy, quickly got out of the car and hurriedly followed the maid. The maid opened a door at one end of the verandah. There was a staircase and the two climbed up. They entered a small courtyard across which was a large well-furnished room. The floor was covered with a white sheet on which was a carpet with bolsters on it. On the walls were ugly, coloured pictures and very large mirrors. On one side was a large bedstead enclosed in a mosquito net. On the other side was a small wooden divan. On this too was a white sheet, carpet, bolsters and other things. There were silver spittoons everywhere. Incense sticks placed on the corners of the carpets drenched the room with scented smoke. On another divan were a silver washbasin, soap dish and dishes of lentil powder. On the carpet, next to the bolster, was a gold and silver betel box. On the other side of the bolster was an ebony perfume box. On a table, in the corner of the room, covered with a patchwork green cloth, was a tray. Flowers and leaves, painted in a variety of colours on the walls and ceiling, hurt the eyes. There were also two coloured glass chandeliers hanging from the roof. The maid, followed by the girl, entered the room. She gestured to the girl to sit on the wooden divan, turned around and left.

With a smile the girl looked around the room. She was amazed by everything. She went to the divan and sat down, her feet on the floor. Almost immediately, she bent down and touched the ebony perfume box, then straightened up. She looked all around to see if anyone was watching. She bent down again and stroked the carving on the box.

The Nawab Sahib was watching from a room across the courtyard. He came in, laughing. 'Yes, apply the *itr*, go on. It's there only for you.' The girl sat up, looked at him and smiled softly.

The Nawab Sahib came forward, saying 'What a ravishing smile you have.' He moved closer and extended both hands to the girl. Instantly, her smile disappeared. Delight was replaced by obstinacy. Obstinacy was quickly replaced by worry and then signs of anger appeared on her face. She was now standing still, staring angrily at the white-haired old man. The Nawab Sahib said, 'All luxuries will be provided for you here and you now belong to me,' and again extended his hand to her. Quickly, the girl stepped back lifted both her hands and began to scratch her face. Then she pulled at her shoulder-length hair, threw it at the Nawab Sahib's feet, and for the first time uttered a sound. *'Aawawa aa! Aawawa aa!'*

The Nawab Sahib froze in horror. In front of him was an angry, ugly fourteen-year-old deaf-mute girl making strange sounds. She rubbed her face hard with her hands; her rouge disappeared in patches and her own dark complexion showed up in spots. Across the right cheek was an unsightly scar which ran to her ear. Another scar with sparse hair decorating it, shone in the middle of her scalp.

She had no father or brother. Who was there to care about that loathsome-looking girl in Daliyabad? However, everyone was concerned about the mare. Once they were in Kanpur, each tried to become the one who would replace the girl. Affection, coaxing, scolding, punishment, nothing worked, for these were the very same people who had stabbed her thousands of times daily with a needle since she was a foal, to make her fearful of all humans. They would bring her into the ring, change into different costumes, come close to her and prick her with a needle. She knew that as long as she was tied to a post she was safe. The moment she heard sounds or was taken away, she knew that anyone who came near her, except the girl, would try to stick a needle into her. She hated all humans from her gut. Her natural instinct of affection contracted and became concentrated on the girl. That young, voiceless animal was eager to express love like a lover and was ready to be loved like a beloved. She would stand silently, jerking her head and whisking away flies with her tail, waiting for that one being—the girl who could not speak.

Without a tear in her eyes or a complaint on her lips, the mare now stands with her front and hind legs both bound. Sometimes she eats a few mouthfuls of hay and then becomes still again. Her ears pressed forward, jerking her head downwards, her tail continuing to swish, she stands silently. Her silence symbolizes her waiting and her hurt, with more waiting to come. All kinds of cruelties were inflicted on her. She was thrashed constantly. Repeated attempts were made to mount her, but she did not give up. She continued to wait for the girl. Only she and no one else would ride her. How could she let anyone else touch her? Even when fetters were put on her legs and a muzzle on her mouth, she used her large muscles to shake off anyone who tried to ride her. Cruelties continued to be inflicted on her. When they tired of this, they would bring her back to her post and tie her up and she would again stand silently; no tears, no sound, no cold sighs, and no pleas. Silence! The only voice of the voiceless, silence! Occasionally, she shakes her head or flicks her tail and she stands there silently.

The circus people thought of punishing her by starving her and giving her a purgative. But she herself had stopped eating. Her body developed sores from being beaten and thrown down. Her heart was in anguish, missing the girl. Her eyes searched for her all the time, forgetting both hunger and thirst. External wounds and internal pain soon transformed the mare. The throbbing, twitching, healthy, gleaming young black mare turned into a half-dead, dirty, dark, plucked, tattered old horse. Flies clung to her legs and gathered around her eyes. She barely moved her tail. She was in a very poor state. Eventually, when the circus was ready to leave Kanpur, the mare was auctioned. The circus manager earned thirty five rupees and the mare departed. She was soon forgotten, for why would anyone want to think of her? Without the girl, she was nobody's mare. Like grass or rubbish which lies around till it is blown or swept away in a storm, these two too had been put out to sea and the ocean tossed them around. One drifted to the east and the other to the west. Only rocks, free of a heart, can sit patiently on a hill for centuries.

Winters pass and springs come and go. So do centuries, races and generations but rocks sit still and watch. And we, twigs in a storm, are tossed and battered, soaring only for a few moments. We, cursed by fate, carry around a throbbing abode of love, passion, despair, hope, desire and expectations called the heart. If circumstances bring us together, we are moved. If tragedies separate us, we reconcile ourselves to separation. The girl did not have a home or family. Her life in the circus was nothing but an early-morning dream. Once awake, nothing of it remained. For the mare, life was now a cart and the lanes and bye-lanes of Kanpur. For the girl there was the stove, utensils, grinding stones and serving two wives. She had to grind the spices, scrub the pots, cook the food, feed the entire household, eat the leftovers and then repeat this all over again.

Years pass. The girl sits on her haunches, holding the grinding stone with both hands, rocking back and forth, making a paste of turmeric, coriander and chilies. Her heart, the damned heart, however, can only think of the circus, the black mare, the loving looks the mare gave her, the mare's curved neck, her beautiful forehead, the way she turned her head to look, the way she quivered and moved, how she fed her hay and grain, rode her, performed acrobatics on her back and the amazement with which thousands watched them. And then the clapping! The world stared and was amazed. That was life. That was life's peak. However other eyes saw none of this nor did ears hear it. Concealed from people, hidden from the world, these memories which couldn't be forgotten or erased continued to haunt the voiceless girl. They came to her whether she was blowing into the stove to light a fire with damp wood or scrubbing greasy, smoke-blackened pots on bitterly cold nights. Year after year, whether shivering in the cold or drenched and panting in the heat, the mute girl thought of those days. But nothing changed. However, the world had changed, and how! She had no parents, siblings, family or friends. She had neither a husband nor a child. How could things change for her? Where could hope or optimism grow? Helpless, hopeless, she continues to live.

Mahmud Ali Khan had been enraged. He had expressed his shame and embarrassment by screaming at the servants, and handed the girl over to Kale Khan, the cook, with the firm instruction that she never be allowed to leave the house. Now the Nawab Sahib's servants behaved with her like their master. There were only two wives in the house. They were worried that this young girl might turn into a co-wife, so they ill-treated her in every way they could. The girl had been handed to them in the bloom of youth. With great skill, these two good housewives started to convert her youth into old age. In a few years the girl had become an old woman. Fifteen years passed with her serving them and getting beaten in return.

Every day we see how in the early light of day everything looks good, fresh and joyous. A moist, cool breeze blows, birds twitter, flowers smile and plants sway. Then, in a few hours, under the blinding sun, everything burns and scorches. The breeze becomes warm and full of dust. The birds hide here and there. The flowers wither, droop and fall. Sunlight and then dust covers the greenery. Nature changes every day. Why is it then surprising that a few days after she was auctioned, the healthy, black, gleaming, pert mare turned into a scrawny animal, yoked to a cart drawing it through the streets of Kanpur? What if she once let no one ride her? Now she has to draw a heavy rattling cart that seems attached to her tail. To sounds of *tukh tukh* and the cracking of a whip, she ferries people from the station to various streets all day and returns home in the evening, exhausted. She gets a lot of rubbing and a little hay and grain. All night mosquitoes bite her and in the morning she is taken out again to raise the dust off the streets. In time, her youth fled but adulthood never came. From a strapping young mare she turned into an emaciated beast drawing an *ekka*.[1]

Yoked and tied, she stood dozing at the station. Passengers arrived. When the luggage had been loaded and the passengers had taken their seats, the *ekka* driver gave two hard tugs, cracked his whip and urged *tukh tukh*. The mare moved her tail and moved her head up and down. She then bent her head down and stood there in a swoon. 'O you mare, may you come to a bad end! Come on, *tukh tukh, tukh tukh*.' The whip cracked again and again. The mare moved her tail, moved her head and her tail again, but stood still. She was then tugged at vigorously. 'O you mare! Move on and may you be destroyed. *Tukh tukh. Tukh tukh*.' Now, exercising her head more than her legs, the mare moved mincingly. The whip was used more frequently. She found it hard to walk.

One day when she was walking hesitantly through the bazaar as usual, she was stopped. She came to a halt and stood there with

[1] A one-horse, high vehicle, peculiar to India.

lowered head. The *ekka* had curtains so two female passengers got in. There was a man with them. The man was Kale Khan, the cook. Of the female passengers, one was a wife of the Nawab and the other, the mute maid. Kale Khan brought some pairs of western-style women's shoes to the *ekka*, put his head inside the curtain and showed them to the wife. She liked two pairs and tried them on. Of the two she told him which one to buy and Kale Khan walked back to the shop. The wife changed her mind. What was she to do? She gestured to the mute maid to call Kale Khan back. The poor thing called out in her tongue, *'Aawawa aawa aa!'*

The miserable old mare heard that voice again after years. It was the same voice that once carried messages of love, the voice to which were linked the happiest memories of her life. When she first heard the voice out of the blue, the mare, startled, laid both ears back and stood still. In the din of the bazaar, Kale Khan did not hear her so the mute girl called out again. The mare moved her ears back again and listened to the voice. Of all the voices in the world, this was the only voice that meant something to her. For years she had longed to hear it again. And for years she had abandoned all hopes of hearing it again. 'This voice! Her voice! The girl is back. I have found her. Where is she? Will she disappear again and I never get to meet her again? What shall I do?' Thoughts such as these may have come to the mare's mind. Who knows what she was thinking? The fact is that when she heard the voice for the second time something seemed to charge the half-dead mare with electricity. She neighed and struggled. Like a deer trapped in a net, she fought and thrashed around. Her harness broke into pieces. The free mare emerged. She started running around the *ekka*. She would stop and rear up. She also kicked with her hind legs, brought her ears together and bared her teeth. But she continued encircling the *ekka*. Hundreds of people formed a ring around her to watch. They were afraid, kept their distance and were ready to run. Among these were the *ekka* driver and Kale Khan. At a distance Kale Khan was seen jumping and screaming to indicate his connection with the covered *ekka* which was now supported by the two wooden bars that had been strapped to the mare. It stood bent over as if prostrating itself while the frightening, wild, black mare circumambulated it, making it clear that she would kill anyone who came near it. The white curtained *ekka* stood silently, the embodiment of misfortune, bent as if in prayer. Still inside the curtains, the wife had fainted from fear. The mute girl moved the curtain aside, and sat there silently, holding the rod of the *ekka*, looking out. Tears flowed down her cheeks. There was now a crowd, a couple of thousand strong, around the *ekka* and near her were the wild hysterics of the mare. The girl saw her old world come alive again. A new spirit ran through her deadened arms and legs. She parted the curtains, jumped off the *ekka* and stood on the road for a moment. And then, in front of thousands of amazed spectators, the ugly, wizened middle-aged woman leapt towards the mare, mounted her and sat on her bare back. The mare galloped off in the direction she happened to be facing. The crowd parted like moss on water and the mare shot through like an arrow and ran through the city.

As if possessed, the old mare kept running, carrying the old woman through crossings, turning corners, avoiding everyone and everything in the bazaar. Neighbourhood after neighbourhood passed and she kept running. The city came to an end. Now she raced on the long straight road to Kalpi. The two travelled for miles. Five, then ten, then fifteen miles passed and two innocent voiceless travellers reached their real, sacred destination. The same destination that all of us travellers in this world are heading towards. After fifteen miles the galloping mare staggered. She stumbled and fell on her face. Her head was smashed. The mute woman was flung ten yards from the mare onto the tarred road and broke all her bones.

Do not be sad, dear friend. This was the sacred moment for which the two had lived their lives apart, so long. What else had there been for them? Who else was there for them? What was there for them to live for? Their youth had been plundered and their adulthood trampled upon. In old age, they would have departed for the other world, alone. What if it was only for a few minutes, at least they were together again. Once more they got to play the game of their youth which they were still playing when the curtain fell.